POWER PLAY

Austin Aces

C.M. KANE

COPYRIGHT

Editing & book design by Maggie Kern @ Ms.K Edits

Cover art by Kristin Barrett @ K.B. Barrett Designs - www.kb-barrettdesigns.com

Austin Aces Hockey Club... where sworn enemies become lovers… on and off the ice.

Join eight of your favorite ✎ romance authors and get in on the action...

One Touch by Linden Rowe https://books2read.com/onetouch

Unleashed by Jenna McCall https://geni.us/yNLnmG

Slapshot by TL Hamilton https://books2read.com/Slapshot-AustinAces

Tripped Up by Allie Lasky https://books2read.com/u/bM8L6X

On Thin Ice by Rebecca Norinne Caudill

Puck Drop by Andie Bale https://books2read.com/u/4NnyOG

Power Play by C.M. Kane https://books2read.com/AustinAces-PowerPlay

Goalie Interference by Kim Findlay https://books2read.com/u/492kwW

DEDICATION

For the players we love to hate, the players we hate to love, and the players who are both pieces wrapped up together in one person.

CHAPTER ONE

E mily...
You can do this. This is what you've trained for your whole life. Now, get in there and claim your future.

As far as pep talks went, it was okay. Trouble was, I was never very good at hyping myself up. But this was my chance to prove what I could do. How hard could it be to get an interview? Sure, he'd never granted one by choice, and he avoided the press like we were lepers, but I could be persuasive. I wasn't above using my looks to get me what I wanted. It wouldn't be the first time.

"Ma'am," the security guard said as I went to enter the locker room.

"Press," I said, holding up my badge.

"Sorry," he replied, pushing the door open to let me in.

The cacophony of voices hit me as soon as I crossed the threshold. A handful of other press were talking to players, but the one I wanted to snag wasn't around.

At first, I thought I'd missed him, that he'd left before the press was let in. It was a tactic he'd used before. Just as I was ready to give up, he walked out of the showers and over to his locker. It was now or never. I had to catch him off guard. I unlocked my phone and opened the app I'd downloaded specifically for this. There was an audio-only as well as an audio and video one. I clicked the record button and headed to him.

"Mr. Johannsen," I said, and he turned to me, looking like I'd just pissed in his Cheerios. "Can I ask you a couple of questions?"

He looked down at my phone, then up at me, and promptly dropped the towel he had around his waist. I caught the movement in my peripheral vision and wanted to look. I *really* wanted to look, but kept eye contact with him, and he smirked.

"What?" he asked, and my mind just went blank.

One, two, three. Breathe. Focus.

"You can count," he said.

"What?" I asked, confused.

"You just counted to three," he said. "Can you count higher? Or am I supposed to be impressed with that?"

His tone was flat, almost mocking, but it broke whatever spell I'd been under.

"Sorry," I said. "You had seven penalties tonight. Was that intentional?"

What the fuck kind of question was that?

"I have no problem doing the time," he said. "Not that they were all warranted."

"You think the refs were wrong?"

"They got a few right," he said.

"Which ones?"

"You really want me to answer that?" he asked, the smirk growing. "Or are there other things on your mind? You know, since I'm standing here naked and all."

I blinked slowly, looking up at his face. Realization dawned on me. He hadn't moved since he'd dropped the towel. I'd been so focused on what I wanted to ask him that I hadn't recognized the reality of what had happened when I first started this interview. Closing my eyes, I took a breath, then opened them again.

"I'd just like to be the one to get an interview," I said. "You're so elusive."

"For a reason," he replied.

It seemed we were coming to an impasse. I couldn't find the right question to get him to answer, and he refused to answer the questions I did ask him. Then there was that stupid smirk on his face. He knew exactly what he was doing, which just pissed me off more.

"So," I said, pushing ahead. "The refs were giving you penalties without cause. Let's go through them. In the first, you were called for cross-checking. I saw it. It was a good call."

I couldn't keep the challenge out of my voice. I wanted to push him for some reason.

"Like I said," he replied. "There were some good calls."

"Same period," I said. "Hooking against Gregor as he was driving to the net."

"Had to stop him," he said.

"Do you have an excuse for everything?"

"No," he said. "I have a reason for it."

"Splitting hairs," I replied.

"I'm done," he said and turned away from me.

"I'm not," I challenged.

He stretched down and picked up the towel, tossing it into the bin near him, then reached into his locker and pulled out his pants. He'd effectively dismissed me, ending the conversation. There really wasn't much I could do without making a scene, so I turned around and left the locker room, shoving my phone in my pocket. Hopefully, something I got would give me the boost I needed to break through and get the on-air spot I'd been craving.

CHAPTER TWO

S   ilas...
        Chick was brazen. I'd give her that. She didn't even
        flinch when I dropped the towel. She also didn't auto-
matically look, either. That put her above most of the press I'd
dealt with. I did interviews when I had to, but didn't like it.
The press shouldn't even be allowed in the locker room. We
didn't need a fucking audience when we were changing.

She'd turned the video on with the app she was using,
which meant she had a clear view of my cock the whole time.
I don't think she realized she'd done it, but at least I was a
shower. I was a grower, too, so if the opportunity came, I'd be
sure she knew.

"Hanny," Keaton shouted. I looked over at him and he
said, "The fuck was that?"

I shrugged, then finished pulling on my slacks. It was still
too hot to be wearing much, so I was as dressed down as I
could be while remaining within the league's dress code.
Why we had to wear a fucking tie and jacket when we
walked to our cars would never make sense to me. But rules
were rules, and you played by them or had to pay the conse-
quences.

When I finished dressing, I headed out of the building to the parking garage. There was a reason I didn't talk to the press. Everyone knew the story. The way they treated my dad when Mom was killed was bullshit. He deserved to grieve in private, to mourn away from prying eyes. The team and the league wanted to showcase that players were more than just on-the-ice madmen. That they had lives outside the stadium.

They were fucking parasites, trying to gain exposure and fame off someone else's tragedy. He deserved better. Mom deserved better. At least they spared me, but it still fucked me up. From that point forward, I vowed to make it as difficult as I could for the vultures who called themselves press.

I was so up in my head that I didn't even notice her standing beside my car until I was almost there. Stopping about five feet from her, I glared. How did she know which car was mine? Let alone when I'd come out.

"You could have said something," she sneered. "But you probably thought it was funny, didn't you? Fucking up my shot at getting my break."

Oh, she was pissed. Like, full-on-rage coming-at-me pissed. And she was sexy as fuck, too. Her tamed waves from earlier were starting to frizz with the heat and humidity, her eyes wide, and her nostrils flaring. My cock twitched with the thought of pinning her against the door of my car, body check style, where she didn't even see it coming.

But too many people were around, so I had to play nice. Of course, I knew what she was talking about, but I'd be damned if I let her off the hook easy. No, I was gonna play with her for a while, see how far I could push her before she broke.

So, I turned on the "Johandsome" charm they'd dubbed me with on social media, smiling big and letting the icy persona fall away. I could be nice when it suited me.

"I have no idea what you're talking about," I lied.

"The fuck you don't," she barked, her eyes full of fire.

"Such a dirty little mouth," I said, low enough so she was the only one who could hear me as I took the last few steps up to her.

Her chin dropped, a shocked look came over her face, and she opened and closed her mouth like a fish out of water. Just watching it made me wanna fill it, which caused my cock to rise to the occasion. You don't shit where you eat, but damn, what I wouldn't give to take her for a spin.

"I tell you what," I said, just a few inches between us. "You come with me back to my place, and I'll give you a much better interview than the last one."

"Fuck you," she seethed through clenched teeth.

"We can make that happen," I replied, my voice still low and only for her ears. "You've seen what I bring to the table… or the wall, or the bed. Your choice."

It came so fast I didn't have a chance to stop it. The slap rang through the lot, bouncing off the posts and walls. The look on her face when she realized what she'd done was perfect. And when I pinned her to the car, her wrists in my hands, my body against her, face so close I could smell the mint from her mouthwash, she stilled, eyes wider than before, breathing hard as she tried to gain some control of herself.

"That one was free," I growled. "Next time you do that, you're gonna get a spanking."

I know I shocked her, could smell the fear on her, feel the pulse quicken under my fingertips. Fuck if I didn't want to take her right then and there.

CHAPTER THREE

E mily...

Everything that had happened in the last few minutes felt so wrong. And yet, I was more hot and bothered than I'd been in months. My ex, Gregory, was a jack-ass, and turned me off men for a good while. It wasn't that I wanted to give up on men altogether, but taking a break was something I'd needed to do. Then, Mr. Asshole of the team decided to show me how a take-charge guy could flip my switch, and damn if it didn't turn me the fuck on.

Still, there was no way we could be anything to each other. Fraternizing with the team was strictly prohibited, especially for someone who was trying to get in front of the camera. Why did it have to be him, though? I mean, some of the other guys were way nicer and knew how to downplay things. Not Johandsome, though. Oh no. He'd take this all the way to where it would fuck me six ways to Sunday, and not in the good way, either.

"Can you get off?" I asked.

"You gonna help?" he asked.

"You're such an asshole," I said.

"Oh, I know," he replied, still holding me against his car.

"Let. Me. Go," I said, emphasizing each word.

"Why?" he asked, shifting his hips so his cock, which was much larger than it had appeared in the video I had, and hard as one of his hockey sticks, pressed against my belly. "You got somewhere you need to be?"

I squeezed my thighs together, trying to gain some control over the situation, only for his eyes to widen a bit, and that fucking smile to grow.

"Me thinks thou doth protest too much," he said, his voice so low I almost missed it. "I think you used the video on purpose, and now that I've called you out on it, you're embarrassed. You got caught, so you're trying to make excuses. Don't worry, babe. I won't tell anyone else. Promise."

"You are such a fucking prick," I growled, squirming to get out of his grip. "Now, let me fucking go."

"As soon as you admit the truth," he said. "You're just as turned on right now as I am. You want me, and it's killing you."

"My fucking God," I said, tilting my head back. "You're so arrogant you think every woman wants you. Let me go. Now."

The last word was said through clenched teeth, and I couldn't tell whether my anger or arousal was the higher emotion. Whatever it was, I needed to get away from him because nothing good could come of this.

"You'll come around," he said, leaning harder against me. "They always come around. Just don't be so shy next time. Ask for what you want. You just might get it."

He pressed a kiss to my lips, so chaste it was a surprise, then stepped back, giving me space to breathe and move. But I didn't. I had to try to gain some control over myself, because he was right about one thing. I was turned on. I did want him. I also knew my career would be over if I went down that path, and Silas Johannsen was not a man to be trifled with. His reputation as both a lady killer and a brawler on the ice was not unfounded, and sometimes those two images clashed. No, I needed to get the fuck away from him as fast as I could. I just had to figure out how to move without falling over.

Mustering every ounce of poise I could find, I pulled away from his car, walking past him toward the building. Just as I passed him, he mumbled something under his breath.

"What did you say?" I asked, turning to him.

"*För ditt personliga nöje,*" he said, and I blinked.

"The fuck does that mean?" I asked.

He smiled, winked, and turned to get into his car.

"Fuck," I muttered, walking back to the stadium.

There was no way I would remember the words he'd said, nor would I likely be able to figure out what it meant without going back to him. And that was something I was going to try to keep from happening, if at all possible. Much as I wanted to be in front of the camera, and getting an interview with Silas Johannsen would've probably gotten me there, I wasn't gonna tempt fate again. I'd come so close, too.

CHAPTER FOUR

S ilas...

Driving home with a boner fucking sucked. But I just had to deal with it until I got back to my place. Pulling into the garage, I shut the door, got out of my car, and headed inside. I dropped my bag on the washer to deal with after I dealt with my dick, which was still waiting for pretty miss interview girl to get on it.

The house was bigger than I needed, but I liked having all the room. It wasn't like I had a family or was planning one. I didn't want to subject a kid to what I went through growing up. Being the child of a professional athlete could be a nightmare, and things were worse now, what with social media and every fucking person having a camera on their phone. Sure, we had to do our duty to the team to post on social media, but I'd never subject a child to it. Still, knowing that there was enough space to spread out, to find some peace away from the rest of the world, that's what I really bought the place for. Besides, I liked having a trophy room. Too bad I hadn't gotten the chance to put the ultimate trophy in there... yet.

I walked into the master suite, which was right at the top

of the stairs, and kicked off my shoes, I set them into the rack in the walk-in closet, then hung my jacket up before dropping the rest of my clothes into the hamper. The house was exactly what I wanted when I went looking, and to have it fall into my lap at the right time was pure luck.

There were things I wanted to change about the bathroom, but making a bigger shower area was the must-do, so I had that remodeled before I moved in. I could have entirely ripped the whole thing out, including the closet on the other side of the bathroom, but it wasn't like it was needed. Getting the shower features that I wanted was sufficient. Maybe someday I'd build my own home out in the middle of nowhere, and my bathroom would be the stuff of legends. Until I hung up my skates, though, I had to be close enough to not have a commute from hell.

Walking to the controls inside the shower feature, I pressed the button for the preset I'd set up. While the water warmed, which didn't take long with the tankless water heater, I grabbed a towel and robe and dropped them on the heating unit just outside the tiled feature. Did I need a warm towel and robe? No. The weather was still warm, but the air conditioning in the house made it chilly enough that I liked the luxury it offered.

I stepped under the spray, letting the water wash over me, and thought back to the game and the after-game interview the sexy brunette tried to get with me. She'd asked about the penalties, and yeah, I'd had a few. Most of them were good calls, but there was one in the third that pissed me off. They called a high stick when mine was well below my shoulders, and the other guy was taller. At least it didn't cost us the game.

Still, the sexy reporter coming up to me and not batting an eye when I dropped my towel… she was good. I hadn't seen her before, though, so I didn't know who she was or who she worked for. Might have to do a little digging to see if I can figure it out. Much as I would love to dip into that sweetness, though, I knew better. I'd fucked that up once, and learned my lesson but good.

Closing my eyes, I remembered how she felt as I'd pinned her between myself and my car. Just the right give in all the right places, but her fierceness was tempting. Fuck, I could smell her arousal like a pheromone drawing me to her. All I wanted to do was lift her leg on my hip, press my cock against her, and see what sounds I could draw from that filthy mouth of hers.

Just the thought of that made me hard again, and I grabbed my cock, stroking it while I thought about all the ways I'd like to defile that beautiful flower. Fill her mouth, fuck her cunt, slide into her ass. God, it was like she was a wet dream come to life, and I lost my load with just a few strokes, painting the walls of my shower with the result. I finished washing myself, then toweled off and tucked into my robe to head down to the kitchen to grab some post-game fuel before heading to bed.

CHAPTER FIVE

Emily...

"Emily," Micah said as I walked back into the arena. "Joe's looking for you."

"Shit," I muttered. "Is he pissed?"

"When isn't he?" he asked me.

"Fair point," I replied.

Heading toward the press area, I passed several players and staff, praying I hadn't fucked up so bad I'd be out of a job. Joe Davidson thought he was the best of everything there was when it came to the sports reporting world, that women should be seen and not heard, and his asshole tendencies were well known at the station. I knew I'd have to come up with a reason why I wasn't at his beck and call when he wanted.

"Ms. Jacobs," I heard, and I swallowed. He didn't sound happy at all. "Now, please."

"Of course," I replied, walking toward him.

"It's come to my attention that you were trying to get an interview in the locker room," he said. "Want to explain that?"

"I saw an opportunity to get an exclusive," I explained.

"That's not your job," he said. "You need to be doing your job, not out there freelancing and getting up in the players' faces."

I didn't say anything, because he hadn't asked a question. Still, I didn't know what my status was with the station. Maybe I'd never have to be anywhere near Silas Johannsen again, and I could forget how he made me feel with his body pressed against me.

"Don't let it happen again," he finally said.

"Of course," I replied, waiting to be released.

"Get," he said. "I want to wrap up the rest of the crew and get out of here."

I didn't need more incentive, so I turned and headed toward the press box where I had left my bag. By the time I got there, the on-screen crews were just wrapping up, so I waited for the camera to be turned off before I moved closer to grab my stuff.

"Hey, Emily," Matt said when the light went out. "How did the interview go?"

"You heard?" I asked.

I'd worked with Matt and Jonah since I came to the station. Both were good guys, but they worked hard as well. I liked them both because they reminded me of my brothers, who were older than me and protective.

"I think everyone heard," he said with a laugh.

"God," I said. "It wasn't supposed to go like it did."

"You got him to at least answer a question," he said.

"Too bad I didn't get anything proving that," I replied, because there was no way I was going to let anyone know I'd filmed his dick.

"Yeah," he said. "That is a shame. Would have done a bit to boost your image, that's for sure."

"It was the only reason I went in there," I said as I picked up my bag.

"Did he really drop his towel and stand there naked while you talked to him?" Jonah asked.

"Yeah," I said as I rolled my eyes. "I think he was trying to see if he would get a reaction out of me."

"Good for you for not giving in," Matt said. "Bet that felt good to be able to actually ask questions and have him answer."

"His answers were vague at best," I said. "Anyway, I'm heading home, unless you guys need something else."

"I think we're good," Jonah said.

"See you tomorrow," Matt said.

"See ya," I replied, then headed out to my car.

By the time I reached my car, most of the others in the lot were gone. Thankfully, I didn't think anyone saw what happened between Silas and me while we were talking earlier. As I slid behind the wheel of my car, I realized that I needed a redo of what I'd done earlier. He'd offered me the opportunity to come to his place for another interview, and as much as I didn't want to admit it, I'd thought about taking him up on that.

Still, it couldn't happen at his place, or mine, for that matter. Fuck, I didn't think there would be anywhere that we could be alone, because all that would come out of it would be rumors of me sleeping with him to get the interview, which would do the exact opposite of what I wanted.

I parked in the garage for my condo, got out, and headed to the elevator. The ride up was quiet, what with it being late and all, and when I keyed my way into my unit, I sighed, tired from the day. I hooked my keys on the hook by the door, took my bag to the bedroom, and undressed to take a shower. The smells of the stadium always stuck to me, and showering before climbing into bed was an absolute must.

As the water started to warm, I undressed and dropped my clothes on the floor to deal with later. I climbed over the tub's edge, grabbed the detachable showerhead, and then pulled the plunger to let the water coming out of the head have time to get to temp before replacing it in its holder. I let the water run over my hair, my hands moving the strands around to make sure it was all wet. I grabbed the shampoo, pouring a healthy amount into my palm before rubbing it into my hair.

Rinsing the suds out, I wondered what Silas was doing. The way he'd pressed me against his car was fucking hot, and I speculated he was that way in the bedroom as well. Why my mind went there was anyone's guess, but I figured it was because it was the most action I'd had since dumping Gregory. Shaking my head, I tried to dispel the thought of the great and powerful Silas Johannsen, but he just kept coming back to my mind.

I poured some of my body wash onto the scrubby I had hooked on the wall and rubbed it along my body. With each swipe of it across my flesh, I tried to remember whether his hands were rough or smooth, but I couldn't bring back the texture. Still, the thought of roughness made me hope they were, figuring the handling of the stick on the regular gave him some callouses over time, even though all the players wore gloves during the games. How my mind kept going back to him made no sense, but I couldn't help it.

Giving in to my baser instincts, I let my mind go to where it shouldn't, and moved my hands along my body as if they were his, caressing my curves, sliding between my legs, pinching my nipples, and anything else I could think of. At some point, I dropped the scrubber and let my fingers slide between the folds, slipping one, then two inside me. My thumb circled my clit as I raised my leg onto the ledge of the tub, and I found that rough patch just inside me, scraping it enough to push me over the edge, and I imagined Silas calling me a good girl as I came.

The rippling aftershocks kept me holding the emergency bar on the edge of the shower wall until I had more control. I let the water rinse the suds from my body, then pulled the handle from its caddy, switching the spray to the pulsing option, lowering it to spray against my most intimate parts, washing away the suds and other fluids from me. Damn if that didn't give me another shiver of delight.

Finally, after getting myself back together and rinsing the suds from my body, I shut the water off and grabbed the towel from the rack next to the tub. Drying my hair first, I wrapped it in the towel, then pulled the second one from the rack to dry my body. When I was fully dried, I hung the towel from my body over the shower rod and pulled the one off my hair, rubbing it thoroughly before flipping it over it.

I pulled the leave-in conditioner from the cabinet, spraying it into my hair, then scrunching it up with my hands, before grabbing a comb to run through it. Each knot that pulled made me shiver, wondering what it would feel like to have someone use my hair as a handle. None of my previous boyfriends were very adventurous when it came to sex, so I had to live vicariously through the fictional characters I read about.

My mom had called them trashy romance novels, but there wasn't really anything trashy about them. They had sex, and I think that was what made her use that term, but it wasn't like porn where there was no storyline. Still, sometimes I wondered whether real life could ever be like it was in the books.

By the time I crawled into bed, I was revved up again, and pulled out my battery-operated boyfriend from the drawer in my nightstand. Closing my eyes, I envisioned Silas. I had actual video of his dick, so could feed that imagination with the reality of what I'd seen. The fact that I could feel he was bigger when he pressed against me told me he would be a tight fit if we were to go there.

I imagined how he would start, whether he'd be soft with his touch or push hard from the beginning. Knowing what I did about him, I figured he'd go full on right from the beginning, so I used my toy to simulate what I suspected would be his style, punishing my pussy while still working my clit with my fingers. Having already fallen over the cliff, the second orgasm hit me faster than usual.

Either that or the thought of Silas pushed me fast, and I didn't want to give him that much power. But I couldn't lie to myself like that, and knew that it was imagining him with me that gave me a faster climax. Maybe I would see about getting that interview, and whatever else he might want to offer me. Because if the fictional him did me like it did, the real one would be a fuck ton better.

CHAPTER SIX

Silas...

I worked hard during the morning skate, which was noon by the clock, to keep my mind on what I was doing, not wanting to be off at all when it came time for the game. Problem was, my mind kept drifting back to a certain brunette who tormented my dreams all night. If I knew who she was, or who she worked for, maybe I could figure out how to get her out of my system, but I hadn't been able to find her anywhere. Fuck, I didn't even know her name.

Out of nowhere, I was slammed into the glass. When I settled back on my skates, the biggest fuckwit on the team was laughing at me.

"Dude," Doyle said through his laughs. "You gotta keep your mind on the ice. You're probably still thinking about whatever wet hole you stuck your dick in last night."

"Keep my dick out your mouth," I barked at him. "Unless you're gonna suck it."

"Fuck you," he said. "I'm not a fucking cock gobbler."

"Don't worry," I said, giving the asshole a glare. "I doubt anyone would want you. If you're not gonna offer, keep it out your mouth."

"You're a fucking asshole," he shouted.

"Damn right I am," I said. "I also know when to shut the fuck up, unlike you."

With that, I turned, picked up the puck I'd been shuffling down the ice, and curved myself around the back of the net to head up the other side. Fucking asshole knows we don't go full contact at the morning skate, nor do you fucking hit someone on your own fucking team that hard, ever. Next time he does it, he'll lose some teeth at best.

The rest of the day went without any issues, mostly because Doyle kept to himself and as far as fucking possible from me. I think a couple of the other guys warned him off because he was distant the whole time. Probably a good thing, too, 'cause one word would've likely ended in bloodshed.

Dressing for the game, I thought about her again, and fuck if I didn't need to focus on ugly grannies to get my dick under control. Unfortunately, it didn't work well, and getting myself ready was a struggle.

"Hey," Keaton said. "The fuck was with dickhead this morning?

"My guess," I said as I finished lacing my skates. "He's looking to start a fight. He thinks he can take my spot on the first line or something. Who the fuck knows?"

"Steer clear of him," he said as a warning. "Something ain't right about him."

"No shit," I said as I got up.

Most of the guys on the team were decent, and I got along with a good number of them. You had to trust your team on the ice to have your back. They all knew I had theirs, except for Doyle, who seemed to be one of the guys no one liked. He wasn't even that good of a player, and I wondered whether he was a charity hire or if he'd sucked the right dicks to get the spot.

Walking to the rink, we passed the local broadcasters as

they were heading up to their box at the top of the arena. Wouldn't you fucking know it, but there was my dream girl, following behind them, chatting about all the shit she needed them to know before they went on the air. When she looked up and saw me, she did a stutter step, her words faltering, but she caught herself quickly and kept on walking.

I saw the color rise from her chest to her cheeks, and knew it wasn't just some imagined thing. Oh, no, she got off to me last night, and damn if it didn't just make me wanna make it happen for real. Still, not gonna shit where I eat. It wouldn't do much to me, but it could destroy her. I was an asshole, there was no doubt, but I did understand how the world worked, and I wouldn't fuck her over like that.

The lights came through the tunnel as we got closer to the ice, and my focus shifted, as it should, to what was going to come in the next hour of play. Viggy slapped the stack of pucks as he went through the bench onto the ice, scattering them around for the rest of us to pick up and work through our pre-game warm-up, just as any good captain would. Soon enough, we'd be hitting, slapping, and scoring goals.

"I'VE HEARD BETTER chirps from a dead bird," I shouted at the asshole who was barking from their bench.

We'd struggled through the first period, but now that we were in the second, we were hitting our stride, with Bell scoring two goals. The kid was quick on his skates, snaking between players like he was born with them on his feet, and damn if I didn't wanna move that fast.

The buzzer went off to end the period, and I hadn't been sent to the box once, which was odd for me. Trudging back to the dressing room, there she was, standing by the local station's backdrop, holding the microphone for one of the guys waiting for an interview with someone who wasn't me. She caught my eye, raised her brow, and watched as I walked right past her. Something was on her mind, but I couldn't read her well enough to know what.

"Dude," Doyle said as I passed him. "Why ain't you hitting?"

"Fuck you talking about?" I asked him.

"Gotta get some actual action going out there," he explained. "You haven't been in the box yet. Don't you get cash every time you go in there?"

"Shut the fuck up," I said, passing him to my locker. "Fucking tool."

I tossed my shirt into the space, turning to sit on my stool. Every fucking time he opened his mouth, bullshit came out. Didn't matter what he was talking about. It was just a bunch of noise that no one wanted to listen to.

"You okay?" Keaton asked.

"Yeah," I said. "Just Doyle being an asshole, per usual."

Coach came in just then and started in with the plan for the third period, talking strategy and plans of action, all of which I should've been paying attention to. But the only thing I had on my mind was that perky brunette and all the things I wanted to do to her. The look she gave me when I first passed her before the game said she'd been thinking about me, and the one she gave me just now said she wanted to talk. Normally, the fact she was press would keep me away, but I was tempted to hit that if I could.

"…needs to hit more," I heard, and knew it was about me. "You gonna get your ass in gear and start crashing the boards more?"

"On it," I said.

"Good," Coach replied. "You've been slackin' the first couple of periods. Need to step up."

"I'm happy to jump in," Doyle said, and I gave him a look that told him to shut the fuck up, which he did.

"I got it," I said, looking back at the coach.

"All right," he said, looking around at the rest of the guys. "Conny, keep it frosty in the crease. Viggy, keep pounding. Bell, get that hat trick."

At that, the entire team let out a whoop as we gathered our gear to get back on the ice and finish this thing.

CHAPTER SEVEN

E mily...

I hadn't planned on seeing him at all, but it wasn't exactly easy to avoid him with as small as the arena was. Still, passing him in the hallway as I walked with the crew before the game startled me. Then, when he walked by after the second period, I gave him a questioning look. Not sure what I was hoping for, but the way he sized me up, I felt the caress of his eyes like they were his hands. I'd be lying if I said I wasn't curious as to what that would *actually* feel like.

Nope, not gonna go there. Can't go there. I like doing what I do, and if I want to move up and get in front of the camera, I can't let him entice me into anything other than the professional connection we've already got. It's bad enough I've got video of his dick, which I did save to a very secret folder within an area in my phone that no one can access without several steps of security. Not gonna let that go to waste, since he was already a dick about it.

The guys were done with the interview, and I was gathering the rest of the stuff we needed to keep secure until the game was over, when the guys started coming out of the dressing room and heading back to the ice. I ignored them, doing my job, trying to be as inconspicuous as possible. When I stood up, I was pressed back around the corner, a gloved hand over my mouth.

"Don't scream," he said, and I instinctively raised my knee to his crotch, hitting his cup, which still did some damage because he pulled off me. "Fucking bitch," he growled, and then he was just gone. I had to blink a few times before I realized that he was on the floor, and I was being pulled back into the light where all my gear was.

"You good?" Johannsen asked, and I nodded, not exactly sure what all happened. "Don't worry about him. Get gone."

He didn't have to tell me twice. I grabbed the things I needed and headed away from both men toward the closet we used for storing stuff between periods, then made my way up toward the press box.

"Hey," Micah said, then added, "What the fuck?"

"What?" I asked, turning to look in the mirror that was just inside the door. "Shit."

"What happened?"

"Just a player being handsy," I said.

"It wasn't the guy you tried to interview, was it?" he asked.

"No," I said. "He actually took the other guy out."

"Girl," he said. "You have got to be more careful. These guys are big, and they ain't afraid to use their muscles to get their way."

"I'm fine," I said, although the girl looking back from the mirror most definitely wasn't. "It was nothing."

If I kept saying it, maybe I'd believe it. Passing the rest of the press, I squeezed into the little bathroom they had in here and locked myself in. I had to bite my lips together to keep from crying out, because I had a fucking handprint across the lower half of my face. There was no way I would be able to say who it was that did it, which was just another thing I had to deal with. One of those guys tried to grab me. His intentions were clear, and thank fuck Johannsen was there. While my knee to his groin backed him up a bit, it wasn't gonna take him down, and there was no way to know what he had planned, or how much he'd've gotten away with if he hadn't been interrupted.

I turned the water on, letting it cool, and splashed some on my face, hoping it would take the redness away. I also wanted to make sure it wasn't obvious that I'd cried, because fuck those guys. It was hard enough as a woman to get any respect in the sports world, but if I was a fragile thing that needed to be protected, it was gonna make it way harder to get to where I wanted to be. Sure, women were starting to see a climb in places, but the way Joe Davidson did things, it would be a cold day in hell before anyone without a dick was in a position that meant anything other than glorified secretary.

Looking in the mirror again, I realized there was no way to fix what the asshole did with his glove over my mouth, so I thought I'd just use it to my advantage. I'd go out there, show them that someone tried to fuck with me, and that I won, or at least got away. No need to tell them someone else knocked the dude out to get me out of the situation. Nope, not gonna tell that little part of the tale. I dried my mouth off, opened the door, and stepped out of the bathroom.

"You okay?" Micah asked as soon as he saw me.

"Fine," I said. "Just wanted to see if I could make this go away. Guess I'm stuck with it for now."

"Do you not have any makeup with you?"

"I do," I said. "But it's too much trouble. Might as well wear it as a badge."

"I suppose I should see the other guy, right?"

"Don't look at their faces," I said with a wink, then looked down at his crotch so he understood what I meant. When he flinched, I sort of laughed a little. "Yeah."

"Good for you," he said. "Show them who's boss."

"Well, it ain't me," I replied. "I just work here."

Heading back over to where I had my gear, I got everything ready to go in order to get the after-game interview, as well as all the stats and such, so the guys on air could look like they knew something. My job was to make sure they looked good, whether it was real or not. Davidson said he wanted people to believe they cared, even when they really didn't know what the fuck they were talking about.

"BELL," I said as he headed toward the dressing room. "Can you do an on-air interview?"

"Sure," he said.

He stepped in front of the backdrop on the wall for this specific thing, handing me his helmet. His mouth guard went in, along with his gloves, and then he took the headset I gave him. Micah aimed the camera at him so he was in view, and I saw the light on the top go on, so I knew we were live. I couldn't hear the questions he was asked, but he answered them clearly, talking about the three goals he got in the game, what it was like when the buzzer went off the third time, and all around about what he thought the teams' chances were for the season. I always hated that last question, especially this early on.

Just as the light went off, I felt someone's hand on my ass, and I turned around, expecting it to be the jackass who'd grabbed me earlier. Seeing Johannsen, his sweater and pads off, sort of threw me.

"Call me," he said, smacking my ass, then walked away like it was a sure thing I was gonna do just what he said.

Bell smiled at me, probably seeing what his teammate did, then headed into the dressing room to finish up the after-game. Shaking it off, I started gathering the equipment to get it all put away before we finished for the night. Micah was surprisingly quiet the whole time, and I wondered what was going on with him. I'm not usually nosy, but his demeanor had changed drastically after the interview started.

We got the equipment stowed, then headed back to the press booth to gather our personal stuff before leaving for the night. I wanted to ask what was up, but didn't want to push him in any way, so just let him figure his own shit out. I had enough to think about without adding his issues to mine.

CHAPTER EIGHT

Silas...

I checked Doyle hard to the ground when I saw how handsy he was with the reporter, then told her to get gone. When he got up, he glared at me like he thought he could take me.

"Bring it," I said, settling myself.

"Fuck off," he replied, brushing past me to get to the ice.

I was glad I'd come back to get my mouth guard. Otherwise, there was no telling what he would've done to her. She definitely needed to pay better attention to her surroundings, especially if that dick was around. Next chance I got, I was gonna drive him into the glass so hard he'd be seeing stars for months. Grabbing my mouth guard, I headed back to the rink. The fact that Doyle was being a fucking pussy about a split lip made me laugh.

Skating around our end of the ice, I worked the drills, getting myself back to where I needed to be once the puck dropped. I got into my zone, found my quiet place, and let the shushing of the skates on the ice ground me. I could tune everything else out—the crowd, the shit talking of the players, the PA system announcements, and the music. Just that slow *shush-shush* of my skates as they slid along the ice, cutting lines in the smooth surface as I made my way around the back of the net and headed back toward the blue line.

The only sound I would be able to hear would be the whistle from the ref letting us know we needed to get back to the bench to start the next period. When it came, I did just that, sliding over to the bench, bringing the puck I'd been working with me, then bending and picking it up to toss into the bucket.

"Let's go, guys," Coach said. "We're up, but only by one. I want hits, goals, and a hat trick for the kid."

The rest of the guys sounded their agreement, and then we headed out to our spots for the final twenty minutes of the game. Puck dropped, and Viggy slapped it back and over to me. I caught it on my blade, scooting up toward the line, passing it off to Silver, who drove it across and around the end. Working our play, we let the puck fly between us, watching for that shot on goal.

When their center slammed Viggy into the boards with a cheap shot while his back was turned, all bets were off. I flew to his defense, dropping my gloves and stick along the way, punching him square in the mouth before grabbing his sweater to yank him back for another blow. I kept pounding him until he went down on the ice and the refs pulled me back to keep me from dropping on top of him.

There was no noise during the entire battle except the grunts from myself and my foe, but once the refs pulled me back, I realized that several other players were getting handsy as well. It did me some good to know that we all had each other's backs on the ice. Picking up my gloves and stick, I headed to the penalty box, knowing I'd have to serve time. Didn't matter to me, though. As long as Viggy was good and none of the other guys were hurt, we'd be fine.

"Austin, number thirteen, has a five-minute penalty for fighting," the ref said as I headed into the box. "Seattle, number seventy-four, game misconduct for checking from behind and fighting. Seattle, number forty-five, five minutes for fighting."

I was glad the asshole who hit Viggy was tossed, 'cause I'd've finished him off when I got out of the box if he hadn't been. We scored two more goals, and the kid got his hat trick. Add to that the win, and it was good enough for me. Walking to the dressing room, I saw the reporter setting up for interviews just outside the door.

She and I needed to have a conversation, but it wasn't something I wanted to do at the stadium. When I got to my locker, I pulled down one of my cards I kept in case I needed to slip someone my number without it being awkward. It wasn't anything fancy, just a plain black card with my number written in white.

Pulling off my sweater, I dropped it and my pads in my locker before heading back out to where she was set up. The light was still lit on the camera, and Bell was answering questions coming into his ears from the headphones he was wearing. I waited until the light went off, then slid the card into her back pocket. She turned to me, eyes wide, and I patted her butt.

"Call me," I said just loud enough for her to hear me.

Walking back to the dressing room, I started the arduous task of removing all the gear I wore to keep me from getting more bruises than I needed from the sport I hated to love. My dad had put me on skates as soon as I was stable enough to handle it. I've got pictures of me before I was two, skating on the rink with my dad's team, tiny stick in my hands, grinning ear to ear. Teenage me rebelled a bit, but when I realized chicks loved professional athletes, and that I could bang anyone I wanted just because I played the game, I worked my ass off to get better than my dad.

Grabbing my towel, I headed toward the showers, needing to get the sweat off me. I also wanted to get out of the stadium without having to deal with the team's biggest dick. Unfortunately, he was under the spray of one of the showerheads. Hoping I could get in, get clean enough, and get out, I ducked under one on the opposite side from where he was. I was rinsing my hair when I felt the snap of a towel on my ass. Without even thinking, I reacted by snagging the end of it and yanking.

"Fuck," Doyle cried as he came crashing into me. "What the fuck are you doing?"

"Defending myself," I replied as I shoved him away from me.

He fell backward on his ass, and it was like steam was coming out his ears at how pissed he was. I didn't have a problem with a guy touching me anywhere, but I had no love for Doyle, and would be glad to see him traded somewhere far away from me.

"Fucking asshole," he grumbled, his voice coming from deep in his chest.

"I've already told you," I said. "I am a proud asshole. The more shit you try to start with me, the bigger I'm gonna be."

"Yeah," he said, a sneer across his face. "Like the fucking fairy, Stryker."

Much as he needed his ass handed to him, it felt like he was baiting me, trying to get me to react so he could get payback against me. Thing was, I knew it and wasn't gonna bite.

"Why don't you go fuck yourself?" I suggested. "Probably the only action you're likely to get, anyway. Not sure anyone would want to get near you."

"I get plenty of chicks," he said, shifting to standing, favoring his left leg a bit. "Maybe I'll go get that reporter lady. She looks like she might be a good fuck."

Yeah, he was trying to bait me. Just made more sense that I ignore him, maybe talk to leadership about the shit he's pulled. If he pushed too far, maybe we could get rid of him before he did some real damage, not just to the team, but to the players on it as well. Turning my back on him, I finished with what I needed, then turned the water off and grabbed my towel to dry off. The sooner I got out of there, the better it would be for everyone.

I PARKED IN THE GARAGE, closing the automatic door once I was inside, then headed through the door, around the corner, and up the flight of stairs to my bedroom. I dropped my clothes in the hamper and got into the shower, finishing what I'd started at the stadium. After I got done, dried, and dressed again, I headed back down the stairs to get a bottle of wine opened and aerating, hoping she called sooner rather than later.

I had a handful of prepared meals in the fridge, so I pulled one out, checking the instructions on the top, turning the oven on, and setting it on top of the stove before pulling down some plates, glasses, and silverware to set the table. She hadn't said she'd call, but I had faith that I'd given her enough incentive to do so. When the chime went off on the oven, I pulled the cover off the meal, slid it onto the rack, and shut the door, setting the timer according to the instructions.

While I wasn't sure exactly when she'd get to my place, I had a rough idea of how long after the game the press had to stay, and figured I had plenty of time to get the dinner most of the way finished by the time she would arrive. After the table was set, I headed back up to the bedroom and pulled open the drawer in my closet that no one else was allowed to see.

Women didn't come to my home, so all the toys in the drawer were brand new and never used. That wasn't to say I hadn't used the same thing on women, because I definitely had. The ones I kept a copy of were the ones that got the best reaction from the women I'd been with. I wasn't one of those guys who thought women only responded to my dick and nothing else. No, there were some things my body simply wasn't capable of, including sticking my dick in more than one hole at a time.

Selecting a few items from the drawer, I set them in the top drawer of the bedside table, which also held a box of condoms and a bottle of lube. It wasn't a sure bet that we'd end up in bed, but I wanted to be prepared if that's where the night went. Checking everything again, I slid the drawer shut, clicked on the bedside lamp, and headed back out the door, turning the overhead light off.

My phone rang just then, and I looked at it, not recognizing the number.

"Hello?" I asked when I answered.

"You told me to call you," she replied. "So, I'm calling."

I smiled, knowing I had her right where I wanted her.

CHAPTER NINE

E mily...

The parking garage was pretty much empty by the time I was heading to my car, which didn't worry me. It was safe enough, with security around to ensure only those who needed to be in the garage were allowed in. Honestly, all I wanted to do was climb into my car and go home, but there was a business card in my back pocket that was begging me to take it out.

Question was, what kind of question would be waiting for me on the other end of the line? Would he invite me to his place for just an interview? Or maybe it would be to a hotel room, with the promise of keeping it all about talk, but him secretly hoping it would turn into a more physical situation. Of course, he could be just as crass as he was the last time we were in this parking lot and pin me against something hard and fuck with me. Just that thought alone made me pull the card out before I slid into my car.

"Hello?" he answered when the call connected after I'd started my car and hooked the phone up.

"You told me to call you," I replied. "So, I'm calling."

"Where are you?" he asked.

"Pulling out of the parking garage," I said just as I turned onto the main road away from the stadium.

"I'm sending you an address," he said. "You need to come to me, and not share this address with anyone, ever."

"You're trusting me with your home address?" I asked, trying not to laugh.

"I am," he said. "And if you abuse that trust, you will live to regret it."

His tone held absolutely no room for argument, and I realized he'd probably never let anyone know where he lived.

"Okay," I said, keeping my voice serious.

"Good girl," he said, and I couldn't help but squeeze my thighs together.

I got a ping on my phone and decided to pull into the gas station to load it into my phone, allowing my car to display the map on the pop-up screen.

"It says it'll take me seventeen minutes to get there," I said once I'd plugged it in.

"I'll be waiting," he said, then disconnected the call.

"Asshole," I said.

I followed the directions, driving toward the west end of the city. It wasn't exactly the highest-priced area, but it was definitely out of my price range. Hell, I was still renting because I couldn't afford to buy even a condo. Maybe, if I could get in front of the camera, my paycheck would be enough to put some money away for a down payment.

Slowing down as I turned onto his street, I crept along, looking for the address he gave me, pulling into the driveway of a huge two-story home. God, what I might do to be able to live in a place like that. Apparently, I was gonna find out, because I turned the car off and took a deep breath.

"Here goes nothing," I said, grabbing my phone and getting out of the car.

It wasn't terribly late, what with a game start time of five, but it was still getting darker by the minute. Still, nine at night, going to the house of someone you shouldn't be meeting with outside the stadium, was a risk. But maybe it'd be just what I needed in order to get in front of the camera. I wouldn't sleep with him to make that happen because he wasn't the one to make that decision. Not only that, but I wouldn't sleep with someone to get ahead at all.

There was one of those camera doorbells just to the side of the front door. I took a deep breath, then pressed the button and waited, still debating the logic in this decision. He opened the door, and I blinked. He was wearing a black Henley short-sleeved shirt with black jeans, and he was barefoot.

"Well, hello," he said, his voice smooth as silk. "Come on in. Dinner should be ready in about twenty minutes or so."

"You didn't have to—"

"Nonsense," he said, shutting the door behind me. "I asked you here. The least I could do was feed you."

It did smell good, whatever it was he was cooking, so I didn't argue more. Still, it felt a little odd that he would feed me for just an interview.

"Would you like a tour of the house before we eat?" he asked.

"Really?" I asked.

"Might as well," he said. "You're the first person to come here besides my dad and manager, and neither cared to take the tour. It's a nice house."

"I guess I can take the tour," I said. "Give me something more to talk about when we do the interview."

"Sure," he said, but it didn't sound like he was.

We turned left from the front door, stepping into a dining room with a long plank-type table. Each side had a bench of sorts tucked underneath the edge of it, making it appear more like a picnic table than a dining room table. Thing was, it looked like it fit the room, and the owner, so I didn't mention anything about it.

The wall on the other end of the room had a little alcove, and there was a small table with some sort of old ship inside a glass case. It was one of those that had the tall masts and sails. It wasn't something I'd expected to see in his place, but it also didn't seem out of place, either. I crossed the room to get a closer look at it, and I felt him follow me.

"It was my mom's," he said. "She got it from her dad, who loved the things."

His voice was soft, like he was afraid to say something too loud.

"It's beautiful," I said, turning to look at him.

He was looking at the ship, and something in his eyes made me feel like I was intruding on a special moment. When he turned to look at me, the look slid behind the mask he seemed to have in place all the time. But for that briefest of moments, I think I saw the real Silas Johannsen, the one he never let anyone else see.

"Kitchen is this way," he said, turning us toward the doorway we'd passed to get to the ship. Much as I wanted to ask about what I saw, I knew it wasn't the right time, so I just tucked it away for later. I left my purse and phone on the table, not wanting to carry them around on this tour of his.

CHAPTER TEN

S **ilas...**

"Kitchen is this way," I said, directing her away from the ship and all the emotions it brought up.

My dad had tried to get rid of everything that reminded him of Mom after she died, but I hadn't let him do that. I took anything and everything he didn't want and stuck it into a storage unit until I had a place I could keep it. Sure, most of it was crap, but the pictures, the stuff she'd kept from when I was a kid and first learning the game, the awards and scrapbooks and newspaper articles were all things I'd have never been able to replace.

Looking at the timer on the stove, I saw we still had about ten minutes until I had to pull the tray from the oven. It had to sit out before it could be served, and that would give me enough time to throw the salad together for the side.

My housekeeper was a godsend, knowing everything there was to know about nutrition and what I needed, which was well above what I'd initially hired her for. Originally, she was just gonna come in and clean house a few times a week, but she asked if I wanted her to add cooking, or at least preparing meals, to her duties. When I'd asked what she had in mind, she said that she had worked for a family with special dietary needs, and learned how to prepare meals ahead of time, stacking them in the fridge and freezer so they could be used whenever needed.

I'd given her my needs, asked her to make a meal plan, and we'd go from there. What she prepared, and how she set everything up, was like she'd been trained for it. I'd doubled her salary and asked her to prepare meals for one or two people, just in case I might have someone over, as well as one big meal to have in reserve if I had a bigger party. That had been three years ago, and I don't know what I'd have done without her.

Watching the feisty brunette walk around my kitchen, looking at the counters, in the sink, and just overall checking things out, I realized that I didn't even know her name. And now that I realized it, I wondered if I'd even asked her, or if she'd told me. Fuck, it would be embarrassing if I asked her and she'd already told me. I guess I'd just have to look like the ass if that was the case.

"What's your name?" I asked, and she turned to me from the other end of the island in the middle of my kitchen.

"Emily," she replied. "Emily Jacobs."

"Nice to officially meet you," I said.

She turned and walked through the breakfast space and toward the living room. Her hands slid along the arm of the leather sectional that went along the windows that were at the funky angle at the back of the house.

"I'm surprised you don't have a television in here," she said.

"There really isn't a great place to have one in here," I said. "There's another room upstairs where I have one."

"I see," she said.

I let her look around the area, just taking her in as she did. She was still wearing the same outfit she had on at the arena, and I wondered whether she ever wore anything more casual.

Not that her clothes were that fancy, just more professional than what I was wearing. Black slacks that hugged her hips and a burgundy blouse that kept the secrets underneath hidden. Honestly, I wondered what she wore when she went out with friends. When she got to the door that went out to the garage, with the other one that went into the small powder room, she looked at me, her hand on the knob for the garage.

"That's the garage," I said. "And that's the bathroom on this floor."

"I see," she said, taking her hand from the door.

"You don't want to check the garage?" I asked.

"Not really," she said.

She pulled her lower lip into her mouth and chewed on the edge of it. I took a couple of steps to where she was and used my thumb to pull it out, and the shudder that went through her made me wonder whether having her here was a bad idea.

"Would you like to see the upstairs?" I asked. She opened her mouth to answer, but the buzzer went off, and she startled, blinking at me. "I'll be right back," I said.

I went into the kitchen and pulled the food from the oven, then grabbed the salad from the fridge and the three dressings I had available, setting everything on the island so it was ready to go when we were done. "Oh," I said when I saw her. "This needs to sit a minute," I said.

"We could start with the salad," she suggested.

"Afraid you won't be able to resist the bedroom?" I asked.

"Not in the least," she replied, a smirk on her lips.

"Fine," I said, picking up the bowl and walking it over to the nook where I'd set the table. I turned to get the rest, but she'd snagged the dressings and followed me. "I'll get the wine," I said, passing her close enough that my hand brushed against her hip.

Her sharp intake of breath told me she was definitely

feeling the tension between us. Maybe this wasn't the worst idea in the world. I picked up the wine and returned to the small table in my breakfast nook, pouring some into each of the glasses on the table, then set it off to the side, sliding into my own chair.

"I didn't expect dinner," she said.

"I know," I replied, dishing some of the salad onto her plate before adding some to my own. "I just wanted to do something nice for you."

"Without any ulterior motive?" she asked.

"Who, me?" I asked, trying to sound surprised.

"Why didn't you tell me I had the video turned on?" she asked.

"Because I thought you knew," I replied. "It never occurred to me you didn't know."

She rolled her eyes, then looked at the bottles of dressing, picking the vinaigrette to pour on her salad. I waited, then took the bottle from her and added the dressing to my own. Picking up her glass, she took a small sip, her eyes widening at the flavor.

"What is this?" she asked.

"It's called wine," I said, not bothering to hide my amusement.

"Asshole," she said.

"Sure am," I replied.

She picked up the bottle, read the label, then set it back on the table.

"Well?" I asked.

"Not something I'm familiar with," she said.

"It's something my housekeeper picked up," I said. "She's the one who does all my meals, so I trust her when it comes to everything I eat and drink."

"Do you drink often?" she asked, taking a bite of her salad.

"Very rarely," I said. "Mostly a glass of wine occasionally, or a bourbon if the team's out at a bar or something."

"I see," she said, taking another bite.

I stabbed the lettuce on my plate, sliding it through some of the dressing that had slid off and onto the plate, stuffing the forkful into my mouth. We ate our salads in silence, each drinking small sips from our glasses.

"You done?" I asked when her plate was empty.

She nodded, so I picked up her plate and took it with my own to the kitchen to set them in the sink. I'd never dated, but this seemed to be going well. Not that it was a date, of course. No, I had just invited her over to make sure she was gonna stay away from the asshole on the team. Yeah, that's all this was.

CHAPTER ELEVEN

Emily...

It was almost like he'd asked me here for a date or something, what with him feeding me and such. I mean, the house was lovely, the food was good so far, and the wine was well above my pay scale. Still, there was something underlying with him that I couldn't quite put my finger on. He was being almost too nice, which was so far out of character for him that it put me on edge.

"You're not allergic to anything, are you?" he asked when he brought the pan he'd pulled from the oven.

"Nope," I said.

"Good," he replied. He had these two potholders that he kinda flipped underneath it as he set it down between our plates, which impressed me. "It's a lemon chicken thing Mrs. Norris makes. I'm not sure what all is in it, but it's really good."

"And she makes you two servings of each meal?" I asked. "I assume you have guests over all the time."

"She makes me two servings," he said as he slid one of the chicken breasts onto my plate. "Because she knows I love this dish. Besides, leftovers are nice to have, too."

"I see," I said as I watched him dish up his chicken breast, then added asparagus and long grain rice to each of our plates.

"Like I said before," he said as he sat down. "Only my dad and agent have been here. I don't have guests. I don't bring dates here or even have dates. You're the first person I've ever invited to my house."

"You're serious," I said after a bit. "You really don't invite people over? Not even your teammates?"

"Nope," he said, scooping up a forkful of rice.

The weight of all that was a lot to take in, so I stabbed an asparagus spear, hoping it would keep me from saying something stupid. Still, I wondered why I was so lucky to score an invitation to his home when he didn't let people over. Sure, keeping the press and fans out made sense, but even his teammates? I thought they were all good friends, or at least sort of on the friendly side.

"I see your wheels turning," he said, and I looked up at him. "You're trying to figure out why I invited you, right?"

"I am," I confessed.

"Don't you have people you don't invite to your place?" he asked.

"No," I said. "I mean, my friend circle is small, but they're over all the time. At least when I'm around. I have such weird hours that I don't have many opportunities to have people over."

"Same," he said after taking a bite of chicken.

"But the rest of the team has the same schedule," I said, sticking a forkful of chicken in my mouth. "Oh," I said as the flavors from the seasoning on the chicken burst in my mouth.

"Good, right?" he asked, a smile on his face.

"It really is," I said after finishing the bite.

"Now you know why she makes me two servings," he said, smirking.

We continued to eat, neither of us talking further, finishing the food that his housekeeper had made. I'd never thought about it before, but he probably had a strict diet he had to follow, so having someone make all his meals ahead of time made sense. And if all the meals were this good, I'd stick to them as well.

"You done?" he asked as I set my fork on the empty plate.

"Yes," I said. "Thank you."

"Of course," he said, picking up my dish and stacking it on his own.

He picked up the empty serving dish as well, taking them all into the kitchen. I got up and followed him in, just taking in his everyday evening, or what I assumed was a normal night for him. He set the dishes in the sink and turned back, running into me.

"Shit, sorry," he said, his hands grabbing my upper arms to steady me, as mine went to his waist to keep from falling over.

"Totally my fault," I said.

I went to move a step back, but he didn't let me go. Instead, he held me where I was, moving a little closer until our chests were nearly touching. He was taller than me by about half a foot or so, so I had to tilt my head back to keep looking at him.

"You need to watch out for Doyle," he said, and my brain did a little screech, like a record scratch or something.

"What?" I asked.

"He's dangerous," he said.

"I don't know who that is," I said.

"He's the asshole who put hands on you tonight," he said.

His left hand came off my upper arm, the back of his knuckles grazing my jaw where there was likely still bruising from where the guy's hand had been firm around my mouth. I sucked in a breath, not because it hurt, but the gentleness of his move surprised me. His eyes came to mine, and the concern in them sort of stilled my breathing.

"You need to be careful," he said. "I'd hate for something to happen to you."

The moment held for a bit, neither of us moving, just staring at each other. Then my phone went off, and we both jumped.

"Crap," I said, shifting around the other side of the island and heading into the dining room where I'd left my purse and everything.

CHAPTER TWELVE

Silas...
The way she scrambled away from me made me think she was feeling the same vibe I was, and I prayed to every god I knew that it didn't freak her out more. It was freaking me out, but that's because I didn't let people in. Inviting her over was probably the wrong thing to do, but I needed her to know about Doyle and his asshole-ish tendencies. Still, I was playing it pretty fast and loose by letting her into my home. But I didn't think she'd take advantage of the trust I'd given her. At least I hoped she wouldn't.

"Sorry," she said as she came back into the kitchen. "My brother took a bad hit, so my mom wanted to know if I knew anyone who might be at the game."

"Your brother?" I asked, completely confused.

"Yeah," she said. "I've got three. Henry plays baseball in Phoenix, Ben plays basketball in Seattle, and Alex plays football in San Diego."

"So, which one was it?" I asked.

"Alex," she said. "I don't know what happened because I wasn't watching the game, but apparently he got hit pretty hard when he went up to grab a ball."

"Wait, you have three brothers?" I said. "And they all play professional sports? But none of them play hockey?"

"Yeah, so?"

"Why do you do reporter shit for hockey then?"

"Because I'm guaranteed not to run into someone who played with one of my brothers," she said as if it were obvious. "I want to make a name for myself on my own merits, not because I happen to be the youngest sister of one of the Jacobs brothers."

"That's actually admirable," I said, and my impression of her went up just a bit more.

"Well, thank you," she said, doing this little curtsey thing.

"I know what it's like to try to walk in the footsteps of someone who came before you," I said.

"Your dad played hockey, right?" she asked.

"Yeah," I said, not elaborating more.

"Then you get it completely," she said, and again, her image rose in my mind. Not only did she not ask about my dad, she simply accepted that I understood where she was coming from.

"Let's finish our tour," I said. "But first," I added, opening the freezer and pulling out two small containers. "Gotta get dessert warming up."

"Dessert?" she asked.

"Of course," I said, opening first one, then the other container. "Do you like cheesecake?"

"You're kidding, right?" I shook my head. "It's my favorite dessert. But how can you eat cheesecake? Isn't that something you're not supposed to eat? I mean, you have a strict diet and everything, right?"

"Mrs. Morris makes the best cheesecake that fits within my diet," I said. "Trust me, it's delicious, and it won't ruin your sexy figure, either."

"My sexy figure?" she asked.

"Fuck yeah," I said.

"Sure," she replied, rolling her eyes.

"Don't tell me you're one of those women who don't realize how sexy you are," I said.

"You are a professional athlete," she said. "You could have any woman you wanted. The fact that you're trying to butter me up, like I'm gonna jump in bed with you because you said I was pretty, means you've been hit too many times in the head."

"Oh, I'm not trying to get you in bed," I lied, because fuck yeah, I'd do that. "I just don't think you realize that you are a temptation walking around that arena. I'm sure every guy that sees you walking by has to shift his dick to make it more comfortable."

"Bullshit," she said, but I could tell she was wondering if I was lying.

"Wanna see?" I asked, shifting to unbutton my pants.

"No," she said, her eyes looking to the ceiling. "I have a very vivid image of what is going on down there. I do not need a replay."

I laughed, because why the fuck not? She was sexy as fuck, but also had that adorable girl-next-door thing going on. I was sure she wasn't as innocent as all that, but she probably hadn't been with a real man, and if she had, it'd been a while.

"I'm kidding," I said, stepping up to her and tilting her head down to look at me. "Unless that's something you want. Because I can go that way, too. I know how to keep a secret, so you wouldn't get into any trouble with the station."

There was a war raging through her mind in that moment, and I wondered whether she'd err on the side of caution, or throw that caution to the wind and hop right on this ride. My dick wanted the second option, but my brain was mixed. Sure, it would be stupid to hit and quit her, especially since she was always around the team. But something was making me want to hit and stick, and I wasn't sure whether that was a good thing or not. Waiting for her response was killing me, though.

CHAPTER THIRTEEN

E mily...

"I'm kidding," he said. He got closer and tilted my head down so I was looking into his eyes. "Unless that's something you want. Because I can go that way, too. I know how to keep a secret, so you wouldn't get into any trouble with the station."

Was he seriously propositioning me? And was I contemplating taking him up on that proposition? There was no way I should even let it sit in my brain to roll around, but there it was, tumbling all over the place, trying to find purchase to plant itself. But I shouldn't, because if it ever got out, there would be no way to live it down. It would take my barely there career and flush it down the toilet faster than anything else.

I could smell his cologne, a mix of sandalwood and campfire and some kind of spice, and it was doing strange things to me. Before I talked to him, there was no way I would ever even be at his house, let alone contemplating doing anything even remotely intimate. And I was considering it, which was so unlike me that I had to fight against it. But I didn't want to fight it. I wanted to see what he could do to me, and what I could do to him.

"Those wheels are turning," he said, his hand still on my chin. "It's like watching you run through every scenario possible, weighing each one to see if they're worth it."

"Yeah," I said, my voice low, just above a whisper. "I'm finding it hard to come up with a good reason not to take you up on your offer."

His nostrils flared, his pupils dilated, and his mouth opened just a bit, like he wasn't expecting me to say what I did. Then his tongue came out and wet his top lip, sliding along it slowly before going back into his mouth. The whole thing was so sensual that I had to squeeze my thighs together, which he must have noticed, because his lips turned up at the edges. When his hand slid from my chin around my jaw and to the back of my neck, I knew what was coming, and I wasn't gonna fight it. Instead, I leaned into it, raising on my toes to close the distance between us faster.

The crash of our lips started slow, but my hands fisted in his shirt, his other hand sliding around my lower back, pressing our bodies together as he moved his lips, sliding that tongue along the seam of my lips, begging for entrance. Opening to him, I tasted the lemon from the chicken, the raspberry from the salad dressing, and the sweetness of the wine, all mixed together in a flavor I desperately wanted more of.

He moved us, moving me backward. When the table hit the back of my thighs, he lifted me up onto the table top as he slid between my thighs, pulling me so I was right on the edge, his cock pressed against the seam of my slacks, never breaking the kiss.

As our tongues tangled, his hands slid up my back, bringing my blouse up as well, and then he unhooked my bra with a simple flick of his fingers. The warmth of his hands against my skin had my whole body temperature climbing, and I felt like I had too many clothes on. My shoes got kicked off, and my hands found their way to the hem of his shirt, sliding it up and over his shoulders.

When he pulled back to take the shirt off, I could see his lips were swollen, his pupils blown, and a hunger was in his eyes that I hadn't seen before. Reaching a hand over his head, he grabbed the neck of the shirt and pulled it off in one fluid motion, dropping it behind me on the table. Then he was pulling my top off, much the same way, and my bra came off with it, somehow tangled in the fabric.

"My God, you're beautiful," he said, almost like a prayer.

The way he was looking at me both thrilled and terrified me. I wanted him, and it was obvious he wanted me, too. But this wasn't a good idea. The chill from the air conditioner slid across my bare skin, and I knew I needed to get out of there. If I kept on this path, I wouldn't be able to respect myself. It would make anything that came after it feel tainted somehow, like I'd slept my way to whatever the story was that I was trying to get.

"I can't," I said, reaching behind me to grab my top. "I need to go."

He was effectively holding me where I was by the position of his body, so I shoved against his chest. The shock I got when we touched just proved that I needed to get away from him and clear my head. This was at the top of all bad decisions, and I couldn't let it keep going.

"Move," I said, shoving again, and he stepped back.

The icy look on his face told me I was right in running away. It was the look he had when he slammed a player into the boards when he was playing. No emotion at all. Just the stone-cold look of a predator as he watched his prey flounder, waiting to strike when I was at my most vulnerable. And I'd nearly let him do it, too.

Haphazardly, I tried to redress myself but wasn't having any luck. I couldn't figure out how to untangle the fabric to make it resemble something to wear, and it was frustrating me so much that I just crumbled it up and held it in front of my chest. Grabbing my purse and reaching down to pick up my shoes, I headed toward the front door, praying that no one was outside at this late hour to see me escaping disaster half-dressed.

As I turned the knob on the front door, it wouldn't open. I tugged and tugged, but it wouldn't give. I shuddered when I realized he was standing right behind me, his hand above my head on the door, holding it shut. I prayed he wasn't gonna keep me here and do whatever he wanted to me before letting me leave.

"Don't say a word about this," he said, his voice next to my ear, the warmth of his breath caressing my skin, blowing the little fine hairs at the nape of my neck along the skin. "If you tell anyone you came here…"

He didn't finish the sentence, just left it hanging there. The sting of tears at the back of my eyes threatened to spill, but I would be damned if I cried in front of Silas fucking Johannsen. I nodded, but he didn't move.

"I won't," I finally eked out.

"Good girl," he said, and the promise in those two little words made my stomach flip over on itself, nearly bringing up the delicious dinner he'd served me.

The door opened, and I slid out, nearly running to get in my car. It wasn't cold by any stretch of the imagination, but I shook hard as I tried to open my car door. After another feeble attempt, it opened, and I realized he'd followed me out and done it. Biting my lip, I slid behind the wheel, tossing my shoes into the passenger seat along with my purse and phone. I clutched the shirt to my chest, not wanting to feel naked in front of him.

"See you in a couple of days," he said, his voice so close I could still feel him.

Pressing his lips to my temple, he held them there for far longer than necessary, then pulled back and shut the door. I pushed the button to start my car, and it roared to life, scaring the shit out of me. The stupid little bell was going off because I hadn't put my seatbelt on, but I didn't want to let go of my shirt. Finally, I reached over, pulling the strap across my body, essentially holding the shirt to me before putting the car in reverse and sliding down his driveway.

What a fucking colossal mistake it was to come to his house. I had no idea what I was even thinking, because I knew he was just playing me, seeing how far he could push me. How stupid had I been to even think this would end any other way than him trying to get in my pants?

CHAPTER FOURTEEN

S ilas...

I watched her back out of my driveway, her shirt held in place with her seatbelt, and I wondered if I'd see her at the next game. My dick was harder than the ice I skated on during the game, and I wasn't sure a cold shower would be able to fix it. I'd have to use my imagination, like the last time we were in contact, but tonight had the advantage of tasting her, feeling her skin, and seeing some of what she had hiding under the strait-laced clothes she sported around the arena.

It'd have to do for the night, but I'd be damned if I'd let it end there. No, she was gonna be mine, and there was nothing she could do to deter me. I walked back into my house, my cock straining against the zipper of my jeans just begging to be released.

"Fuck," I muttered as I shut the door and flipped the lock.

Being turned down was a new experience for me. Even in high school, anytime I asked a girl out, they jumped at the chance. Of course, it could've been because of who my dad was. By college, I was prepared to sleep with the entire female population on campus and not feel the least bit bad about it. After I was drafted and started up the ranks, women came to me. I wasn't used to chasing someone, but this woman threw all my confidence off track, and I didn't like it.

I checked the stove, shoved the cheesecake back into the freezer, and shut all the lights off before heading up the stairs. I didn't even get her to the second floor before she ran out.

"Pull you're shit together," I said to myself.

Shucking my jeans, I walked into my shower, snagging a towel along the way to drop into the warmer. It was hot as balls still, but with the AC, having the warm towel kept the chill off my body, and my body didn't need any further trauma. I pressed my preset on the wall, punched the button to lower the water temperature, then stepped under the spray, letting it run over my overly sensitive skin.

"Fucking dammit," I grumbled.

She was so responsive to me initially, bringing her lips to mine to start the kiss, then pulling me closer as I deepened it. It was like fire to gasoline, flames flying hot and fast between us. Touching her skin was electric, charging from my fingertips straight to my cock. But her mouth was wild, wet, and tasted like everything I fucking loved. The way she sucked my tongue, sliding hers along it, then delving into my mouth, I would be willing to wager she could suck cock just as well.

Fisting my dick, I thought of her mouth, letting the water from the shower help me stroke myself, imagining it was her mouth. Her dark eyes, like melted chocolate, rolling up to look at me as my cock disappeared inside was all I needed to think about before I lost my load, it spilling from the end of my cock as I continued to stroke.

Once I was spent, I cleaned myself up before stepping out and shutting the shower off. I pulled the towel from the warmer, drying myself off before dropping it into the hamper. If I couldn't keep her out of my mind, it was likely to screw up my game, and I wouldn't have that.

Maybe I needed to get myself lost in another woman, find some puck-bunny who only wanted to fuck a player, and work her over until I got it out of my system. Not tonight, though. Tonight would be the last time I thought about that hot-as-fuck reporter and what she might be like if we were to get physical. When I got up in the morning, Emily Jacobs needed to be banished from my life.

I finished the weight training I needed to do, then headed down the stairs to grab something for breakfast. As I turned the corner at the landing on the stairs, my eyes saw something at the other end of the table in my dining room. Walking over, I realized it was a bra. Not just any bra, but one that belonged to Emily Jacobs, someone I was not supposed to be thinking about anymore.

How she'd ended up getting out of my house last night without her bra wasn't exactly that hard to figure out. I'd pulled it off with her blouse, and it must have fallen out when she picked up her top and left. It was a dainty thing that I didn't really get a chance to look at, what with being in such a hurry to get her naked. Now, though, in the light of day, I wondered whether her panties matched it, and what she'd have looked like prancing around in just the two items of clothing.

Just the thought of her made everything from the night before come back, and damn if I didn't want to find her, pull her to me, and do all the things I'd dreamed about in my fitful sleep with her. But she was off-limits. Hell, she'd been a scared rabbit, running from me so fast she didn't even put her clothes back on. God, I had it bad, because I was feeling some type of way about that, too, and it just didn't sit right with me. I tucked the bra into the pocket of my shorts and finished my trip to the kitchen to get some food in me. That would hopefully help me think clearer.

CHAPTER FIFTEEN

E mily...

I made it to the end of his block, turned toward the freeway, then pulled over on the side of the road, put the car in park, and sobbed. Why had I thought he would be any different with me in his house than he'd been in the parking garage? I had no clue. Maybe I was just a hopeless fool.

When I finally got all the emotions out, I pulled back onto the street and headed to my apartment. I probably should have tried to put my clothes back on, but I didn't want to chance him coming to look for me. At least it was late enough that no one was around when I pulled into the parking garage. The elevator was also empty, so I just held my blouse against my chest until I got into my apartment and shut and locked the door.

Sliding down against it, I had another good cry, reminding myself why dating athletes was a bad idea, and going to his house was at the top of that list of terrible reasons. The fact that he felt comfortable enough to kiss me, strip me, and ogle me was enough. My issue was that I hadn't resisted. If I'd said no or pushed him away, maybe I'd've gotten that interview I desperately sought.

Instead, I dove head long into it, giving as good as I got, and enjoying every fucking second. That is until the chill hit my naked chest and brought me back to my senses. Thank fuck I didn't go farther, because that would have been it. I'd've had to hang up the microphone forever and find some hole to crawl into. God knows none of my brothers would've let me live it down, either. Oh, sure, they'd've said they cared, that they felt for me, but it would forever taint my reputation with them. And I wasn't gonna give Silas fucking Johannsen the satisfaction of ruining me.

Standing up, I gave myself a good talking to, took my cranky ass to the bedroom, and headed to the shower to wash everything that was that man from my body. As the water cascaded over me, I closed my eyes, trying to push thoughts of him from my brain. Trouble was, he was good. At kissing. At cooking. Fuck, even picking a good wine was within his talents. I went in looking for an interview and came out even more confused and frustrated than I had been after my first botched attempt.

I knew he was an asshole before the first time I tried to talk to him. His actions that time proved exactly that. That he was an asshole who only thought about himself. Then he offered what I thought was an olive branch, only it was just another ploy. This time to get me in a place he was comfortable, where I would be off-kilter and at his whims. But I wasn't exactly blameless. No, I went in knowing all this, and it smacked me in the mouth with how epically horrible it turned out.

"Can't change the past," I mumbled to myself, then got on with the process of cleaning myself from the night.

My hair was a mess, the way he'd shoved his hand into it as we'd mauled each other's mouths. He'd held me where he wanted me, which was normally fine. Now, though, looking back at the night, I should have seen everything coming. Polite conversation, showing me around his home, giving me a glimpse into his private life. What I didn't know was whether it was all an act.

Climbing from the shower, I wrapped my hair in a towel before drying my body. I grabbed some pajamas and a clean pair of panties from my drawer. Maybe I should throw the ones I was wearing away. It would keep me from remembering how wet they were when I ran out of his house. Still, they were one of my favorites, and the matching bra did wonders for my lackluster chest.

Getting myself dressed, I tossed the clothes I'd worn into my hamper, only to realize my bra wasn't there. I went back to the front door, but it wasn't there, either. Maybe it was still in the car, but I wasn't about to go out and check now. No, I needed to sleep. Thankfully, there wasn't anything I needed to do for work, so I planned to sleep in, get laundry done, and see if I could figure out a way to forget the night I'd just had.

I went back to the bathroom, put conditioner into my hair, then combed it through before adding some lotion to my elbows. I brushed my teeth, trying to get not just the regular stuff from my mouth, but also to try to banish the memory of Silas. I hated how easy it was for him to get under my skin, not to mention inside my shirt.

"Not again," I said to my reflection after spitting out the toothpaste. "You will not let him get the better of you. Be strong."

That pep talk wasn't any better than the one I'd given myself before I went into the dressing room. Still, I'd keep telling myself that until I started to believe it. Plugging my phone in, I climbed into my bed and prayed I'd be able to sleep.

"You have got to be kidding me," I said as I shut my car door.

I'd checked everywhere in my apartment, then everywhere in my car, and my bra was nowhere to be found. The only thing that made sense was that it fell out of my shirt when I picked it up and ran out of his house. That left me with two options. I could either wish my favorite bra a fond farewell, or I could try to get it back. And I wanted it back.

The question was, how was I going to go about it? I could call him and ask him if I could come get it, or I could just go to his house and see if he would give it to me. One thing I knew I didn't want to happen was to have him bring it to me at the stadium. That meant I had to get it today, so I decided to just go over there. I went back into my apartment, grabbed my phone and purse, and then headed back out to make the trip out to the fancy part of town.

CHAPTER SIXTEEN

Silas...

The pounding on my door pissed me off as I was in the middle of my run, so I tried to ignore it. It stopped, so I continued running, only for it to start up again. Maybe, if I waited long enough, whoever the fuck it was would leave. Instead, it started up for a third time, and I was done. Slamming the emergency stop on the treadmill, I grabbed the towel from the handle, swiped the sweat from my head, and then wrapped it around my neck as I stomped down the stairs.

"This better be a fucking emergency," I said as I got to the door, wrenching it open.

"It is," Emily said, pushing past me to enter my home.

"The fuck you want?" I barked, and not just because she interrupted my workout.

"I left something here last night," she said, barging into my dining room. "I want it back."

I watched as she went into the dining room, looked under the table, then around the back end of it, before turning to me, hands on hips. She was sexy as fuck when she was pissed. I was leaning against the wall at the entrance to the room, and I couldn't help but smirk at her fury.

"What the fuck did you do with it?" she asked.

"I don't know what you're talking about," I lied.

"Bullshit," she said, stomping to me. "You have it some-where, and you're gonna give it back."

With each word she said, she poked my chest. Her nails were polished, but natural. On her last word, though, I snagged her wrist, pulling her body against mine, knocking the breath out of her as I did it.

"Let me go," she said, yanking at her wrist to try to get away from me.

"No," I said, my other arm snaking around her waist.

"You fucking asshole," she shouted, using her other hand to pound on my chest.

"Will you hold still?" I said, holding her tighter against my chest. A sob broke from her, and she sort of lost all her fight, going nearly limp in my arms. "Oh, baby," I said, walking with her over to the table, kicking the bench out, sitting down on the end of it, and pulling her onto my lap. "Come on, now. It's not that bad."

"Says the asshole who's trying to ruin my career," she said.

"I'm not trying to ruin your career," I said, shifting her so I could see her face.

"You didn't tell me I had my camera on when I first tried to interview you," she said. "You invited me to your house under false pretenses, and now you won't give me back my property. And when I call you out on it, you trap me and won't let me go."

"Well," I began, my hand on her knee, caressing it. "In my defense, the first one wasn't my fault. I honestly thought you did it on purpose. The fact you didn't change the angle of your phone told me you wanted video of my dick."

"Why would I want that?" she asked.

"No clue," I said. "Just figured you wanted to get that in your phone. Some people would pay big money for a video like that. How was I supposed to know you were actually looking for an interview?"

The fact that she hadn't stood up or tried to get off my lap meant she was either comfortable with it or didn't realize where she was sitting. I wasn't gonna complain or make her move, though, because I kinda liked it.

"How about inviting me over under false pretenses?" she asked.

"Now that's just not true," I countered. "I invited you over to make sure you knew to stay away from Doyle."

"I completely forgot about that," she said.

"So it wasn't without reason," I added. "And I'm serious. He's not a good guy, so please stay as far away from him as possible. I would think the actions from the other night would make that clear."

"It does," she said. "But I may not be able to avoid him completely. I mean, I work at the stadium a lot, and have to talk to most of the players at some point throughout the season. Avoiding him may not be completely possible."

"Then make sure you have someone with you," I said. "If you have to be around him, make sure your camera guy or another player is there. Hell, just have me be with you anytime you need to be around him."

CHAPTER SEVENTEEN

E mily...

"Then make sure you have someone with you," he said. "If you have to be around him, make sure your camera guy or another player is there. Hell, just have me be with you anytime you need to be around him."

I turned and looked at him, because that just didn't seem like something I could do. I had to meet with the players, set them up for interviews, and give them information so they knew where to be and when. I usually did that on my own. Trying to avoid a player would be nearly impossible.

That's when I realized I was sitting on his lap, and had been since he first grabbed me. His thumb had been sliding over my thigh, just above my knee, the whole time, and I hadn't noticed. Standing up, he let me go without a fight, and I brushed my hands down my backside, like I was trying to get the feel of him off me.

"Your bra is upstairs," he said, standing up. "If you want to finish the tour, you can come with me."

The smirk on his face told me that's exactly what he wanted, but not in a way that would mean I was taking the tour. No, he likely wanted to get me upstairs so he could try to push me into something more intimate, and I wasn't gonna fall for it.

"I'll wait down here," I said.

"Your choice," he said. "But I was gonna let you film it with your handy little phone to use for that interview you wanted."

Now he was just being cruel. He knew I wanted the interview to pursue my dream of being in front of the camera, and he was baiting me with that very thing.

"I promise I won't even touch you," he said.

"If we're gonna do that," I said. "We should probably redo the tour of this floor."

See if he could get out of that one.

"Sure," he said. "But you have to do all the views from within the house. Nothing that will show the outside. I don't want anyone to be able to figure out where I live."

"No problem," I said, stepping to the front door. "I can start right here. Won't even video myself coming into the house."

"And no questions about the stuff I have around," he said. "Like my ship in the dining room, and some of the stuff I have upstairs in my office. Anything that's a national award is fair game. Anything that's not something given to me in either college or the NHL is off-limits."

"Sure," I said, thrilled that he was actually being nice and not the asshole he was last night.

"When we get to the door to my office," he said, waiting until I was looking at him before continuing. "I'm going to have you shut the camera off. I'll take you in and point out all the trophies you can talk about. Then, we'll come out and restart the camera."

"Okay," I said. "Whatever you say."

"Good," he said.

"Did you want to change or anything?" I asked, realizing he was wearing workout clothes and was kinda sweaty.

"Nope," he said. "It's my day off. I do my workout on my day off, so you get what you get."

"That's fine," I said. "I just wanted to give you the option."

"You worried it's gonna look like you ambushed me?" he asked.

"I mean…" I said with a shrug.

"Because you did," he said. "You're just lucky you're cute."

The last was said with a smile, and I blushed. Damn him and his stupid ways. He was the biggest asshole in the world, so why did he have to go and do something nice? It just wasn't fair.

"Will you be willing to do an interview after the tour?" I asked.

"Sure," he said. "Let's get through the tour first. Then we'll see how we feel."

"You're not gonna give me my bra back while I'm filming, are you?" I asked, realizing that might be a possibility, and I definitely did not want that to happen.

"No," he said. "I'm not that big of an asshole. Although the fact that we're both dressed pretty casual, and that I'm all sweaty from working out, might be an indication that we're a little more familiar with each other."

"It'll be fine," I said. "I'll just say that you gave me a call to come right away. That you had time between your workouts and wanted to get this in while you could."

"How did I get your number?" he asked.

"I don't know," I said, exasperated. "I'm not worried about all of that, honestly. I'll figure it all out once I get this all done."

"So," he said. "You're a fly-by-the-seat-of-your-pants kinda girl, huh?"

I rubbed my forehead, wondering whether this was all gonna be worth it in the end. Honestly, it might not be. Hell,

Davidson might not even want to look at the footage. Or, more likely, he'd take the footage and use it, then take credit for it all. How would I prove it was me that took the video, anyway? Fuck, this might all just blow up in my face.

"Those wheels are turning again," he said, and he was up close to me.

"Wondering whether my boss is gonna just take the footage and use it and not give me credit," I said.

"He won't," he replied.

"Who's gonna stop him?" I asked because I really wanted to know.

"Me," he said. "We'll do the tour, do the interview, then I'll contact the station and let them know that I have granted you an all-access pass, so to speak. That you already have the film, and it won't be turned over until I have it in writing that you will be the one to present it."

"You'd do that for me?"

"Of course," he said. "Why wouldn't I?"

"I don't know," I said, because I didn't.

"You really do think the worst of me, don't you," he said. It wasn't a question, but more of a statement. One I couldn't really argue with, either. "I've just never met the right person to be able to try and not be an asshole to. Maybe you've changed me."

I laughed, because that was ridiculous.

CHAPTER EIGHTEEN

S ilas...

She wasn't wrong to laugh at my statement. It wasn't like I had a track record for not being an asshole, or a dick, or whatever other colorful term someone wanted to use for me just not being nice. Still, I hadn't been mean to her on purpose, at least not after that first attempted interview.

"Sorry," she said when she'd finished laughing. "I've just never heard you even try to be nice to a reporter. Yet, here you are, not only inviting me in, but willingly giving me a tour of your house on camera, and saying you'll do an interview. I'm just skeptical, is all."

"Then you don't want to do it?" I asked, knowing that wasn't at all what she wanted.

"I didn't say that," she replied.

"Then let's go," I said.

"Would you mind if I checked my hair before we start?"

"Go ahead," I said.

She walked past me toward the living room, and I heard the door to the bathroom open and close. While she was in there, I ran up the stairs and grabbed her bra from the nightstand, stuffing it into the pocket of my shorts. Taking a quick look around the room to make sure it wasn't in terrible shape, I peeked at the mirror above the dresser to see if I needed to comb my hair or anything before running back down the stairs. I made it down just as she was coming out of the bathroom.

"Did you just run upstairs and do your hair?" she asked.

"I went to make sure my bed was made," I said, which wasn't exactly a lie.

"Oh, really," she said, sounding unconvinced. "Well, then, let's get going."

She went to the front door, opened her phone, and turned on whatever app she was gonna use to do the video. She fiddled around with a few things, then stood in front of the door and pressed a button on her phone.

"This is Emily Jacobs," she began. "I have been invited into the home of Silas Johannsen, first-line defenseman for the Austin Aces Hockey Club. He has graciously given me the rare opportunity to not only chat with him one-on-one, but to peek inside his home. I'm excited to see where he lives, and to chat with him about hockey, and everything else under the sun."

Her voice had taken on a quality I hadn't heard from her before. It was definitely her reporter voice, but it was nice. She pressed her phone again, then pulled it down from in front of her.

"Did that sound cheesy?" she asked. "It sounded cheesy to me. Maybe I'll do it again."

"Nope," I said, my hand going over her phone to keep it down. "It was just fine. I don't have all day to do this, so if you're gonna do it, let's get to it."

She looked at me, then nodded. Raising her phone again, she pressed something else on it before she started talking again.

"Mr. Johannsen," she said, and I looked at the phone.

"Please," I replied. "Call me Silas. Or Si."

"Of course," she said. "Silas. Thank you for letting us into your home. We're not showing the outside to allow him to keep his privacy, but it is beautiful."

"Which was a condition of this interview," I said, making sure that particular piece of information was on the video.

"And one I will absolutely honor," she said. "Anyway, thank you, again."

"You're very welcome, Emily," I said, then watched as she blushed, giving me some type of look from behind her phone.

"The foyer is lovely," she said, tipping the phone up to take in the two-story space. "It's such a classic design. The glass on the staircase is particularly interesting. Did you purchase the home new?"

"It was already built when I moved here and was in a position to buy a home," I said, watching her in her element. It made me wonder why she hadn't gotten a shot to be in front of the cameras. "I did have a few things remodeled before I moved in, but those are upstairs."

"You'll have to be sure to point them out when we get there," she said, turning the camera away from the ceiling and toward the dining room. "Next, we come into the dining room. The table is definitely large enough to entertain at least a few people, but I understand you don't usually have people over."

"As we've established," I said. "I like my privacy."

The rest of the tour continued in a similar manner—her asking questions or making comments, and me either answering or agreeing with them. She didn't open the garage door, stating that she wanted to be sure my car wasn't on the video, which I appreciated.

"Now, I have to say," she said when we finished the main floor. "These stairs are unique. I would be concerned with the glass myself, but I've been known to not be nearly as steady on my feet as you. At least, I assume you're steady, what with your ability to stay upright on those tiny blades you skate around on."

"I'm fairly steady on my feet," I said, walking up the stairs behind her.

I'd let her go ahead of me for a couple of reasons. First, having a camera following me up the stairs wasn't my idea of good television. Second, I'd felt her ass, but didn't get the chance to get much of a look at it when she was at my place last night. And damn, had I missed out, because these jeans hugged her curves the way I wanted to.

"Where shall we start?" she asked, turning the camera toward me.

"Turn right," I said, having gotten my eyes off her ass just in time.

We went into what was supposed to be the family room, but I'd turned it into a workout room. My treadmill, weight machine, and the handful of free weights I had for simple exercises were in here. It had a recessed wall that backed up to my bedroom, where I had mounted a television, with shelves underneath that held a couple of gaming systems. The couch across from the television was comfortable enough to game on for a couple of hours, but I didn't use it much.

"I wondered whether you had a television," she said, even though she knew I did. "You've got a couple of gaming consoles as well. Which ones do you like the best?"

She turned her phone to me, so that what I said would be on the video, not just my voice off-screen.

"I actually don't play that often," I said. "Just in the off-season. During the year, I'm focused on my game, but when the season is over, blowing off steam with a video game is nice."

"I see," she said. "You've got a treadmill and some weights. What is that machine?"

"It's a weight machine," I said, walking over to my stand. "All my exercises are sanctioned by the training staff, and nothing I do here is with anything very heavy or strenuous. I'd hate to get hurt at home and mess up the team."

"That makes sense," she said. "What's the next stop?"

I walked her to the other end of the hall, where I had the guest bedroom and office. She asked about the bedroom, and I explained that my dad sometimes came down to see me. When we got to the office, I could hear her breath catch.

"Let's turn the camera off for a minute," I said, and she did, pressing whatever button she used to start and stop the recording. "I wanted to show you what you could and couldn't take video of."

"Okay," she said, her eyes looking around the room.

"These are from when I was a kid," I said, showing her a shelf of trophies my dad nearly tossed. "If you need help figuring out what they're for, I can tell you, but I'd like to not dwell on those."

"Okay," she said. "Can I do a quick video of them?"

"Let me finish first," I said.

"Sure," she said.

"Some of the trophies I won in college," I said. "As well as pictures and articles from the newspaper about the awards. I'm good with explaining these on camera if you want. And this is the Calder Memorial Trophy."

"What's that for?" she asked.

"And you call yourself a sports reporter," I said with a laugh.

"Hey," she said, looking at me. "I didn't know I was gonna be doing this today. If I had, I'd've looked up everything you ever won and known what they all were."

"I'm teasing you," I said.

"Oh," she said.

"It's the Rookie of the Year award," I said. "It's the only national award I've won since coming into the league."

"Why's that?" she asked.

"People don't like hitters," I said.

"The fans love it when you guys drop your gloves," she said.

"True," I replied. "And it brings in revenue. But the powers that be, the big bosses, try to push that down so we don't do it as much. They don't want us to get hurt in a fight, so they try to make sure that the awards go to those who don't really fight."

"They like you to fight to bring in revenue," she said. "But won't reward you for bringing in revenue by fighting. That makes perfect sense."

"Tell me about it," I said. "But we don't let anyone get cheap hits in, either. Like that one on Viggy the other night."

"What was that all about, anyway?" she asked.

"No clue," I said. "Sometimes, a guy will have a beef with another guy. They'll find any excuse to hit 'em. But Viggy is one of the nicest guys you'd ever meet. I don't know anyone who's got a beef with him."

"Was he hurt?" she asked, and I looked at her. "Oh, right. I would have to ask the brass, wouldn't I?"

"You sure would," I said.

CHAPTER NINETEEN

E mily...

When we walked into his trophy room, I was impressed. The room was lined with shelves on one side. There was a desk with a laptop in one corner, and a couple of overstuffed chairs, but the wall was amazing. He'd asked me to stop recording, then walked through every item on the wall, telling me what I could and couldn't take video of. He also told me what he'd be willing to talk about on camera.

As we continued, he started talking about the politics of the league, which just showed me that the gladiator mentality was alive and well, living in the arenas that housed hockey games worldwide. It didn't surprise me so much as make me wonder how no one else noticed it. After he'd explained his awards, I took some video of the wall itself, then added a couple of shots of the rookie award he received.

"Over here are my personal treasures," he said when I'd finished recording. "My mom was a scrapbooking queen, and she put everything that ever came home with me into one. I'm really glad she did, but it's a lot."

"How old were you when she died?" I asked. "Not for the video. I just want to know."

"I was nineteen," he said. "I was at college, which is how I avoided the media circus right after it happened. It's one of the reasons I don't talk to the media."

"That's just awful," I said.

"It was," he replied. "It damn near killed my dad, too. He got to drinking, then started getting into fights with anyone and everyone on the ice. When Detroit sort of forced him to retire, I thought he was gonna drown in booze."

"I'm so sorry," I said.

"Thanks," he said, and there was a little catch in his voice.

"Do you want to take a break?" I asked.

"Let's finish the tour," he said. "You haven't seen the master bedroom yet."

"Do I want to record this?" I asked.

"Depends on what you plan to do in there," he said, his smirk back.

I rolled my eyes, then pulled the phone up, pressing the button to start recording.

"Last room is your master bedroom," I said, purposefully pointing the camera right at his face. "So far, the house has been very orderly. Most people can keep the common areas clean, but their own bedrooms are where all the secrets lie."

I was pushing, and I knew it, but the playful banter we'd shared throughout the tour made me a bit silly. Never in a million years would I think that Silas Johannsen would have a soft side. It was why I hadn't asked him questions about his awards. I'd seen the struggle he had just talking about what they were. When he started talking about his mom's death and then how his dad reacted, I wanted to lighten the mood.

"Well," he said, looking right at me through the phone. "My bedroom is likely the cleanest in the house."

He stepped from the office and walked to the door at the top of the stairs. I didn't know what I was expecting, but this definitely wasn't it. The double doors opened to a sparsely furnished space. The bed was to the left, and it was simple, but giant. I didn't think I'd ever seen a bed as big as this one.

There was a small sofa and table, with another overstuffed chair in front of the windows with an angular look that matched the living room below it. Everything was in a sage green color, with dark wood for the table as well as the head-board and nightstands.

"This is amazing," I said, unable to keep the awe out of my voice.

The wall to the left of the doors, across from the windows and beside the bed, held a giant painting. It had this remark-able old brick structure on the left, ivy growing up some of the surfaces, with a brick patio-type thing next to it. On the right, going all the way toward the center, you could see either a lake or river, with trees and a lawn of some sort. The colors were vivid, and it looked like sunset the way the sky was flushed with pinks and oranges.

"It is," he said, and had that faraway look I'd seen before.

"Can I get a close-up of the artist?" I asked quietly, hoping the phone didn't pick it up. He shook his head, which made me want to see who it was even more. "Okay," I said, just taking in the larger image in my shot. I'd come back and take a peek after we finished this tour.

"The changes I made are in the bathroom," he said, heading toward a door on the right side of the room.

When I stepped into the space, my jaw hit the floor. My whole apartment could fit inside this bathroom and still have room left over. Straight ahead of me, I could see the closet, which seemed fairly orderly, but we'd see once we got in there. To my left were some cupboards with a sink before the giant tub that looked like it could hold three or four people without any trouble.

On the right was a door that I assumed was where the toilet was, since I didn't see one in the rest of the room. I didn't open the door, not wanting to expose a stinky space if he hadn't cleaned it. Past the walled-in area was a shower with glass running the entire length. I could see a showerhead on the wall at the end of the bathroom, but there was one on the side wall and another one on the ceiling.

"Three showerheads?" I asked. "What did you change?"

"The shower," he replied. "It was pretty small, and there was an extra sink and counter here," he continued, pointing to the end next to the toilet. "I wanted a bigger space, along with a bench."

He pulled me into the bathroom farther, and I looked into the shower. There were showerheads all along the wall against the toilet, which baffled me. Like, why would someone need all of that? It made no sense to me.

"It's amazing how much the pulsing from the shower-heads helps with sore muscles," he said. "It's why I had it changed."

"Oh," I said, feeling stupid. "Can we look in your closet?"

"Sure," he said, stepping in.

I was blown away. The built-in cupboards and such around one end were all made of the same dark wood that the furniture in the bedroom was made out of. On the other wall, along the back of the bathroom, there were rods to hold his suits, as well as more drawers. Everything was neat and orderly, and I wondered whether he hated disorganization.

"And that's it," he said.

"Thanks," I replied, turning the phone off and sliding it into my back pocket. "I'll have to charge it before we do the sit-down. Do you want me to bring my own in or do you have one I can borrow?"

"I've got one," he said, guiding me from the closet with a hand on my back.

His touching me did things to my body I didn't like, because I didn't want to have any reaction to him. It was bad enough last night when I'd completely lost all control over my faculties, but I needed to be professional. Especially when I put all the footage into a video to submit for broadcast.

"Here," he said as we got to the bedroom. "You can leave it here, and we can get something to drink. I need to hydrate."

"Oh, sure," I said, plugging my phone into his charger.

He headed out the door, so I took the chance to look at the signature at the bottom of the painting on his wall. It was kinda hard to make out, but it looked like an M and a T before his last name. I couldn't remember his dad's name, but I somehow didn't think it was his work. I figured it was something his mom painted.

"Coming?" he asked, sticking his head around the corner.

"Yeah," I said, stepping from the painting to follow him down the stairs.

CHAPTER TWENTY

S ilas...

"Coming?" I asked her when she hadn't followed me out of my room.

"Yeah," she said, standing up from inspecting the name at the bottom of my mom's painting.

We went down the stairs, and I pulled out a couple of tall glasses, filling them with ice and water from my fridge. I set them on the island, then opened the fridge to pull out a plate of fruit that Mrs. Morris fixed up when she was here last. She always made sure that I had both fruit and veggies available all the time, which was extremely convenient. Emily had picked up the glasses and taken them to the tall table we'd had dinner on the night before, so I headed in as well, setting the plate between us.

"My mom painted it," I said as soon as I sat down. "That's what you were trying to figure out, right?"

"It's what I figured," she said. "I understand why you didn't want me to get the signature. Before I send everything in, I'll have you look at it and make sure I didn't leave anything you don't want in there."

"I'm sorry, what?" I asked, confused at her words.

"The videos from today," she said. "I'm going to put it all together, along with the interview we'll do once my phone is charged, as an episode for the station. I won't turn any of it in until you watch it, though."

"Oh, right," I said. "You gonna be able to get the interview with just your phone? Don't they usually have one on the person doing the interview, one on the person being interviewed, and another aimed at both of them?"

"Normally, yeah," she said. "I do have a second phone I could use, so we'd have you and then both of us."

"Don't you want one pointed at you?"

"No," she said. "It'll be bad enough having it on both of us. I didn't exactly come dressed for this."

"You're saying you don't always go out to interview people in jeans and a T-shirt?"

"Very funny," she said, picking up a piece of watermelon from the plate and popping it in her mouth.

I grabbed a piece of cantaloupe and did the same thing, relishing the fresh burst of flavor on my tongue. Having her in my house wasn't as weird as it was last night. It almost felt comfortable, which was strange because I'd never thought I'd live with anyone once I bought my own place. Of course, thoughts of the night before also brought up the fact that I still had her bra in my pocket. Pulling it out, I set it next to the plate of fruit.

"Oh, thank God," she said. "It's my favorite."

"Did you wear matching panties last night?" I asked, not able to stop the smartass remark from coming out.

"Asshole," she said, but there was a smirk on her face.

"Guilty," I replied.

She took another piece of fruit, this time a strawberry, biting the end of it off, juice slipping down her chin. Without thinking, I reached over, swiped it up with my thumb, bringing it to my lips, and licked it off. When I looked back at her, she had her bottom lip between her teeth, her eyes wide, looking at my mouth. When her tongue came out and licked her bottom lip, my dick stood up to pay attention.

"You keep doing that, we're not gonna get any interview in," I said.

Her eyes snapped to mine, a blush coloring her cheeks.

"We can't," she said, but there wasn't really any heart in the words. It was almost like she didn't really want to say it.

"Says who?" I asked.

"Are you kidding?" she asked, this time with force. "I will not sell my body to get in front of the camera, so if that's what you want, I'll just leave."

"I promised you an interview," I said. "I don't go back on my word. I also told you that I wouldn't tell anyone if anything happened between us."

The war waging behind her eyes told me everything I needed to know. She wanted me, but she didn't *want* to want me. Funny thing was, I didn't want to want her, either, but I did. And not just for a quick fuck, either.

"Can I be honest with you?" she asked.

"Yeah," I said.

"Don't let this go to your head," she said, and I nodded. "Since you're the hardest player to get an interview with, I thought if I could get into the dressing room and surprise you, I might get just enough of a sound clip that I could use it to make the station take me seriously."

"And because I dropped my towel and didn't tell you that you were taking video, I fucked that up," I said, knowing it was the truth.

"So," she continued after taking a sip of her water. "When you told me to call you and then sent me your address, I thought maybe you felt bad for what you did."

"Now that you're here," I said. "You know I did it on purpose, right?"

"Yeah," she said.

"I'm sorry," I said, and she looked at me. "I just thought

you were some puck-bunny looking to get with one of the players. I didn't know you were actually a reporter."

"If you knew I was a reporter?" she asked.

"I'd've just turned my back on you and waited for you to leave," I said.

"But you're letting me video your home," she said. "And sitting down to do an interview. Why?"

"Because you're not asking the wrong questions," I said. "You're considerate, kind, and you're not pushy. I mean, you are, but not in a bad way. It's the first time someone's actually asked me questions that matter. Asked permission before bringing up topics everyone else just bulldozes over. You respected my request to not do something, not talk about something, like my parents, my mom's death, and all the shit that surrounded that time. You're not treating me as a commodity that you're owed a response from."

CHAPTER TWENTY-ONE

E mily...
"You're not treating me as a commodity that you're owed a response from," he said, and the reality of his life kinda just became clear to me.

"Today has been really eye-opening for me," I said. "I think what really struck me the most was when you were talking about the awards they give out for the league. Made me think of Rome and the gladiators they forced to fight for the entertainment of the people."

He scratched his chin, and I could tell he was thinking about what I'd said.

"Before you respond," I said. "And I hate to be like this in this specific moment, but can we grab my phone before we continue? Or yours? I just know that this information, this conversation, really needs to be had on a broader scale."

"Normally," he said, a smile coming to his mouth. "I'd accuse you of using me. But I think you're right. This is something I'd like to talk about."

"Good," I said, getting up to run upstairs to get my phone. When I get to the side of the bed, I see that it's only at about thirty percent, which means it's not nearly charged enough to do the interview. "Shit," I said.

I turned around and ran right into Silas's chest. His arms wrapped around my waist, holding me to him as my hands fisted in his shirt.

"It's a slow charger," he said, his voice low, the rumble in his chest vibrating against mine. "I forgot to tell you, so I knew it probably wouldn't be ready."

"Okay," I said, my voice low.

"I need a shower," he said, not letting me go. "You asked about the shower, so I thought I'd show you what it can do."

"Does that line work on women?" I asked.

"Never tried it," he said. "But I'm hopeful it might work on you. You know, since I've been so gracious to give you the tour and interview and all."

The crooked smile made him almost look like he was innocent, but I knew better. In just a couple of days, he'd weaseled his way under my skin in a way I never expected, and I honestly didn't know what to do.

"You should stop thinking so much," he said. "Let go and have some fun. I promise I won't hurt you. Unless you ask me to, that is."

I tried to take a deep breath to get my bearings, but that was the worst thing I could've done. The musky smell of him invaded my senses, and all I wanted to do was give in and let him do whatever he wanted with me. Then I thought about everything I'd been through, the way that Mr. Davidson looked down his nose at me when I said I was working on an interview. The way that player, Doyle, felt like he could just grab me like he did, and all the other shit I'd gone through in the last few months. In that moment, and sure that he'd show me a really good time, I gave in, nodding to him.

"Is that a yes?" he asked.

"It is," I said. "Show me how that shower works."

His lips crashed against mine, his hands splitting with one

going down to grab my ass and the other to slide into my hair, and he ravished me with his mouth. Opening for him, I let him take control. I relished in the fact that he knew what he was doing, which was such a far cry from the last few boyfriends I'd had, who seemed to only think about their own finish.

"Come on," he said, grabbing my hand and pulling me toward the bathroom.

He opened one of the cupboards inside the door, grabbed three towels from the shelf, then turned to the shower, shoving the towels into this canister thing before pushing a button on the top of it. Sliding the door to the shower open, he reached in and pressed a button on a panel I hadn't noticed before.

"You like hot, warm, or cool showers?" he asked.

"Warm," I said. "Well, warm to hot."

"Good," he said, pressing another button on the panel. "Get naked," he said, pulling his shirt over his head in one fluid motion. I sort of just stood there, because I wasn't exactly sure how this was gonna go. "Here," he said, helping me pull my shirt over my head, then sort of laughed.

"What?" I asked.

"You have layers on," he said. "In Austin. It's hot as balls here."

"It's October," I said. "It's not that hot."

Shaking his head, he pulled my tank top off, then reached behind me to unclasp my bra. Deciding that two could play this game, I reached out and started to shove his shorts down, but they didn't want to go, and I had no idea why. His hand slipped into the front of them and pulled the tie at the front, letting the waistband loose so I could easily remove them. He'd kicked his shoes off in the bedroom, and when the shorts came down, he sort of walked out of them, kicking them toward the door.

I unbuttoned my jeans, sliding them down my legs, then

had to get my shoes off while my legs were trapped together. He bent down, untying them and pulling them off, setting them off to the side before helping me get the jeans off. We were both there with nothing on our tops, but he had a pair of boxers on, and I had my panties, which were definitely *not* what I would've worn if I knew I was gonna get naked in front of him.

"You wanna go first?" he asked. "Or do you want me to?"

"I've got less on than you," I said.

Without even a blink, he shoved his underwear down, and his cock came free. Damn if it wasn't bigger than what was on the video I had of him.

"Your turn," he said. I looked up at him, then slid my underwear down, letting them fall to the floor. "Damn," he said, looking me up and down. "You are sexy as fuck, you know that?"

"If you say so," I said.

"Oh, baby," he said, sliding a hand along my waist and around my back, pulling me to him. "Whoever it was that made you think you're not the finest thing in this world should be checked into the boards, hard."

His lips pressed against my forehead, and I closed my eyes, letting myself feel for a bit. It had been a while, sure, but I wasn't sure that I'd ever been held like Silas was holding me in that moment. He was so strong, yet I felt he was handling me like I was fragile, and it was kinda nice.

"Water should be ready," he said, steering us into the enclosure. "We'll start with a shower," he said as we got under the waterfall coming out of the thing in the ceiling. "Once I've got you all clean, I'll get you dirty again."

CHAPTER TWENTY-TWO

Silas...

She was fucking perfect. Soft in all the right places. I wanted to just sit and stare at her, but my cock wanted to do so much more. Much as I knew I needed to take things slow, I also wanted to be buried inside her. But I'd told her I wouldn't hurt her, so I had to keep my word. Just diving right in and pounding her until I exploded would definitely hurt her. Maybe not physically, but it would show her that I was just the asshole she thought I was, so I'd hold off on my release until she got hers.

I turned her around so her back was to my front, and she tipped her head up, letting the waterfall from the ceiling soak her hair. Grabbing the shampoo, I poured some out and started working it into her hair, using my fingers against her scalp, massaging her head. When she sighed, I knew I was doing something right.

Stepping back a bit, I pulled her with me so the water could rinse the suds out of her hair, which was darker now that it was wet. I put one arm around her waist, pulling her snug against me while the other worked to ensure I got all the shampoo rinsed away.

"You smell so good," I said in her ear and felt her shiver, which just made my cock jump. "You keep that up and we're gonna finish before we even get started."

"No reason it has to be a one-and-done thing," she said, turning her head enough so I could see the smile on her face.

"Oh, baby," I said, my hand sliding down between her legs. "I don't plan on it just being one. I'm gonna make you come over and over again until you're so exhausted you can't even stand. Then, I'm gonna take you to my bed and start back up."

"Big talk from a guy who hasn't even started anything y... Oh."

The shift in her voice, and the way the last word was stretched out, told me that my finger found purchase between her folds, hitting the bundle of nerves situated at the apex of her sex, and it must have short-circuited her brain. She leaned her head back against my shoulder, her eyes closed, and her mouth hanging open. It took a bit to get us here, but now that she was naked next to me, I couldn't think of a reason to slow myself down, other than to make sure she got off a couple of times before I did. I'd never been a selfish lover and didn't plan to start now.

Holding her tight, I backed up to the bench I'd made sure was included in my remodel, lowering myself onto the tile. She resisted sitting on my lap, so I sat her next to me, then shifted so I was in front of her. Her eyes were wide. She opened her mouth to speak, but I pushed myself up onto my knees, pressing my lips against hers. The resistance softened, then she opened her mouth to me, and I took full advantage.

It wasn't just her mouth that opened for me, either. Her legs parted, giving me space to move between her thighs. I wasn't looking to enter her, yet, but I wanted to have space to get to her core so I could slide my fingers and my tongue into her most intimate part. Some guys didn't like to give oral to women, but it was one of my favorite things. Not just because it got women off, but when they came on my face, I was in fucking heaven.

My hand hadn't stopped its work on her clit, but I had switched it so my thumb was doing that work while I slid first one, then a second finger inside her, slow at first, then picking up the pace. She was frantic against my mouth, one of her hands sliding down to join my own on her pussy, the other one was on the back of my neck, keeping my mouth attached to hers.

Her hips bucked against my hand, working herself up to get over that epic fall we all want. Her pussy tightened around my fingers, little moans coming out around my tongue until she pulled her head back, released my neck, and let out this guttural moan that seemed to come from the depths of her soul. Blinking her eyes, she looked at me, and I couldn't help but smile, because watching her fall apart was beautiful.

"That was…" she said but stopped after the first two words.

"Fucking spectacular," I said.

"What?" she asked.

"Watching you come like that," I said. "God. It was absolute perfection."

"Your turn," she said, trying to move.

"Not yet," I said, my hand on her thigh to hold her where she was. "I wanna taste you, and watch you fall apart with my tongue."

Her eyes widened, her nostrils flared, but she smiled, leaning back and giving me access again.

"Lie flat," I said, helping her to turn.

When she was flat on the bench, I pressed her legs further apart so I could get to her pussy. Leaning forward, I kissed the inside of her thigh, my eyes looking up at her wide blue ones. My tongue slid between my lips, tasting her soft flesh so close to where I wanted to be. Slowly, I nipped and licked my way toward her mound, her breaths quickening the closer I got, until I pressed my tongue to her clit, flicking it.

She sucked in a breath, her mouth opening just slightly, her tongue flicking out in time with my own. As I quickened, so did she, and damn if it wasn't sexy as fuck to see her practically begging me to fuck her with my tongue. Happy to oblige, I dipped into her opening, her taste tangy and sweet, and I couldn't get enough.

Her back arched as I sped up, and I reached up, my palm finding her breast. I rubbed it until her nipple peaked under my palm, then squeezed it between my thumb and forefinger. Her hand came to my head, pressing me into her pussy, my nose pressed on her clit, my tongue delved into her core, and damn if she didn't just let go again.

CHAPTER TWENTY-THREE

Emily...

The second orgasm was better than the first, and it came so fucking fast I didn't have time to prepare myself for it. The fact that I didn't have to do anything other than hold him where I wanted him to be was a bonus. Every other time I'd gotten off had been at my own hand. If he could bring me, not once, but twice, and in such short succession, without even getting his dick involved, I wondered where we'd be once he used that appendage.

"You good?" he asked, helping me sit up on the bench.

"Better than good," I said. "So are you."

"Oh, no, baby," he said. "That was all you."

"It was definitely a first," I said, unable to stop thinking about it.

"First what?" he asked.

"First time I didn't have to do it myself," I said.

"What kind of assholes do you date?" he asked, seemingly offended.

"Apparently the wrong kind," I said, looking down. The last thing I needed was to have him feeling sorry for me.

"Then we need to get you off again," he said, determination in his voice. "Because I'll be damned if I'll let the male population go out like that. It's our duty to make sure our women get off. It's a fucking shame no one's done that for you before."

"What?" I asked him because he wasn't responsible for my exes.

"I'm gonna make you come so many times you won't be able to stand," he said, and I could see he was making that his mission. "I want you so well fucked you won't be able to walk without thinking about me. You need to walk into that stadium tomorrow, and everyone should be able to tell you have been…"

"No," I said, putting my hand on his chest. "I can't go in there with people knowing what we've done. That's why I ran out last night. We can't be together."

"The fuck we can't," he said.

"I need my job," I said, feeling my chest tighten. "I can't live without having a job. Can't pay my rent, buy food, or put gas in my car. None of it. You might have millions of dollars in your bank account, but I'm lucky to have two nickels to rub together."

"You're not gonna lose your job," he said. "If they fire you, I'll make sure the team knows why."

"Because that wouldn't give me the biggest black mark," I said.

"Fuck them," he said, and he looked pissed.

He got up, walked under the shower, and let it run over him. Closing my eyes, I tried to find a way out of this. Silas had been kind to me, kinder than I ever thought he could be. Much as I wanted to stay, I knew I had to leave. Getting up, I opened the shower door and reached down to pull a towel out of the basket thing he had them in. When his arm snaked around my waist and pulled me back, I fought him.

"Let me open it," he said, his voice calmer. He pushed a button on the top, opened the bin, and pulled out the towels.

"They're warm," I said as he handed one to me.

"I know," he replied, wrapping one of the towels around his waist.

I'd taken one of them to wrap my hair up, but he began drying my body with the third towel. His slow movements along my body felt nice. The way he was doing this, taking care of me, felt both amazing and terrible. I hated that I fucked this all up, and all I wanted to do was get the fuck out of here so I could climb into my own bed and cry myself to sleep. Or at least until I felt a little less guilty about it all.

"Stop thinking," he said, wrapping the towel around me. "Everything will be fine."

"Says the man who has no dog in the race," I replied.

"You think it'd look good that I'm fucking a reporter?" he asked. "Everyone knows I hate you guys on principle, so the fact that I'm in a relationship with one would be the end of me."

"Relationship?" I asked, turning to look at him.

He gave me a crooked smile and shrugged. That made no sense, because he was just fucking me as payment for letting me interview him. How had this turned into something else? When did it turn into something else?

CHAPTER TWENTY-FOUR

Silas...

What the fuck had I just done? I said relationship to her. Said we were in one. Fuck, I never did relationships, but there was definitely something here. I'd seen guys get screwed over by women, and swore I'd never let anyone have that much control over me. Yet, here I was, tossing the word out like it was normal. And yet, it felt right.

"We can't be in a relationship," she said, probably for the hundredth time. "I can't be in a relationship with one of the players. Mr. Davidson hates me as it is, especially after the failed attempt at the first interview with you. He'd accuse me of fucking you to get a story."

"Isn't that what you're doing?" I asked, then wanted to kick myself. "No, that's not what I meant. But you came over last night for the interview."

"And that's all I intended it to be," she replied. "I hadn't planned on dinner, or anything else. Even today, my goal is to get my bra back. This," she continued, waving her hand between us, "was never supposed to happen."

"Little late for that, now," I said.

I'd walked her out of the bathroom and into the bedroom,

getting her to sit on the end of my bed. Now, I just had to get her out of her head so I could show her that not all assholes were inept. I also wanted to get inside her. I wanted that almost as much as I wanted to win the cup. And fuck if that didn't freak me out just a little bit.

"Tell you what," I said, leaning down over her. "You get this interview, get your place where it belongs, in front of the camera, and then we make things official. I don't mean that we don't keep this up, because this is definitely a good thing. I'm just saying we keep it on the downlow until you're where you want and need to be."

"Everyone will think I slept with you for the interview," she reiterated.

"Fuck 'em all," I said, pressing my lips to hers.

Her hands came up to my face, and I pressed her back onto the mattress, my whole body leaning over her until she was flat. Then I lowered myself down so my weight was on her, and she gasped, giving me access to her mouth. I fucked her mouth with my tongue while pressing my cock against her body, grinding it against her. When she started moving with me, her legs spreading, wrapping around my waist, I knew I'd effectively shut whatever asshole from her past who had made her think less of herself out of her mind.

Pressing up, I yanked my towel off, dropping it onto the hardwood floor before reaching for hers. She let me have it, raising up enough to get it out from behind her back, then she scooted up on the bed, getting closer to the pillows. Grabbing the towel on her head, she dropped it over the side, her wet hair tumbling around her shoulders.

"Do you know how fucking sexy you are?" I asked, but she shook her head. "Well, I'm gonna show you. I'm gonna worship every fucking inch of your body until you understand that you are a fucking goddess."

"Oh," she said, the word a surprise coming from her lips, like she didn't expect the compliment.

"I'm gonna give you a few more of those, too," I said as I crawled up the bed.

I kissed first one, then the other ankle, then moved up to her calf, kissing along each side as I got closer to her thighs. Passing her knees, I continued up, hitting each side as I passed it. When I got to the top of her thighs, she was wide-eyed, her hands fisting in my duvet, but she didn't push me away, didn't try to keep me from getting to her, no matter what she'd said earlier. She may have said she didn't want this, but her body was telling an entirely different story, one that I was listening to more than her words.

I lowered myself onto my elbows, then hooked a hand under her thigh, shifting her so her pussy was open to me, tilting her pelvis so I had better access. With her leg draped over my shoulder, I pressed an open-mouthed kiss just to the side of her pussy. The resulting moan was what I wanted to hear before I moved over and licked from opening to clit. When she shuddered, it was all I could do to keep from diving right in.

I wanted to take it slow, build her up, edge her a bit, make her want it so much she begged me for release. My asshole tendencies were something I prided myself on when I was on the ice. In the bedroom, I could be just as bad, but there was always a better outcome in those situations.

As her breathing increased, so did my attention to her body. I'd moved to sucking and biting her clit, and slid my fingers inside her, stroking that rough patch every so often. Not enough to push her over completely, but just enough to get her closer. We hadn't really talked about things that were off-limits, so I wasn't sure she felt about the back door. Not wanting to stop the progress with words, I slid my finger through her pussy, then along the taint until I hit the tight hole at the back.

Instead of just going in, I worked my finger along the edges, pressing but not entering. The shiver her body gave as

I pressed told me she probably didn't oppose the intrusion, but I didn't want to go too far and fuck up this ride I was taking her on. Putting just enough pressure on the opening, I scratched the patch inside her pussy, scraping it with my fingernail until she was panting faster, and I knew she was about to go over that edge.

As her pussy clamped down on my fingers, I slid the one at her asshole in just a bit, and she let go of a scream that shook the windows, calling my name like it was the only word she knew. I kept her on that high, stroking her as she convulsed around my fingers, her legs trying desperately to put my head in their vice grip, until she slowly started to come back down.

Pulling from her, I climbed further up, pressing my lips to hers as her legs wrapped around my waist, her arms around my shoulders, and she kissed me with all the intensity of the orgasm I'd just provided her with. Her pussy grinding on my cock made me wish I was already sheathed to enter her, but I hadn't thought that far ahead.

Not wanting to break the mood, I leaned toward my nightstand, pulling the drawer open and grabbing a condom from the open box. She broke the kiss, grabbed the protection, and tore the package open with her teeth. Pulling the disc out, she reached between us and put it on my cock, as if we'd done this a million times before. Once I was covered, she angled me to her entrance, then pulled me to her with her feet on my ass.

I'd hoped to get her off one more time before we got to this point, but she had other ideas, and I wasn't gonna argue with her. Sliding inside her, she felt so tight. I worried I'd need to go slow, but she put her hands on either side of my face and looked into my eyes.

"Fuck me," she said. "Fuck me hard and fast."

"Yes, ma'am," I said, and surged forward, burying myself completely inside.

"Oh, God, yes," she groaned, shifting her pelvis up to meet me. "Do it again."

I pulled back, then slammed into her again, this time with more force than the first.

"Again," she said, her eyes not leaving mine.

Over and over, I surged forward, then pulled back to do it again. Her feet came off my back, and I reached down with one arm, pulling one of her legs up and over my shoulder, giving me a better angle to go deeper. I pounded her pussy as hard and fast as I could, bearing down to keep myself from coming before she did. When she finally arched her back, her head tipping up, and her pussy pulsing around me, I came with a force I hadn't experienced before.

Completely spent, I let myself down, angling so I was next to her, pulling her along with me, both of us on our side. When we figured out how to breathe again, I held the condom to the base of my cock before pulling out of her. The shiver of her body, and the pulse of her pussy told me she was well satisfied.

CHAPTER TWENTY-FIVE

E mily...

He fucked the same way he played hockey, with an intensity and passion that was unsurpassed. I didn't know that I'd ever been as satisfied as I was after he'd fucked me, but I knew that I didn't want to go without that satisfaction ever again. If this thing between us didn't work out, I might have to just keep seeing him for the sex alone.

Shit. I was starting to see this as more than just a good time, and that wasn't something I should've been doing. But what if we could figure it out? It was definitely *not* anything we could broadcast, but maybe we could do like he'd said, keep it on the downlow, out of the public eye. If so, I'd be good with having him fuck me like he'd done on a much more regular basis.

"*För ditt personliga nöje,*" he said, and it reminded me that he'd said something like that when I first confronted him about the video.

"What does that mean?" I asked, running my fingers along his chest.

"It means that I am here for your personal pleasure," he

said. "I will let you use me like this as much as you want, because trust me, it is the best I've had."

"Is that what you said to me when I confronted you in the parking garage?"

"Probably," he said. "It's one of my favorite phrases. My dad hates it when I speak Swedish. He was adamant that I speak English only, but my mom let me learn Swedish behind his back. Mostly, I learned swear words at first, but then I started taking an interest in the language. When Mom died, Dad was banging around the house, swearing, but also saying just these little phrases. He'd say, *'Min älskade'* all the time."

"What does that mean?" I asked, surprised he was sharing this with me.

"My beloved," he said. "He really loved my mom. It almost killed him when she died. Not just the drinking and shit, but the fights and everything. His teammates tried to keep him safe, help him keep his shit together. Finally, the owners stepped in and made him take time off, which ended up being the end of his career."

"That must have been so hard on him," I said. "And you. I can't imagine what my dad would do if my mom died."

"It fucked us both up," he said, finally tipping his eyes up to look in mine.

The pain I saw in them was just... I didn't know. It was immense, powerful, and overwhelming. He was still a teenager when she died, and he had to deal with all that, and his dad falling apart. It must have been a terrible thing. I placed my hand on his cheek, my thumb stroking his bottom lip, and let him be. I didn't push or ask questions, just let him experience whatever it was he was dealing with and waited him out.

I'd never experienced a loss like that, but I could empathize. My parents were alive, even my grandparents, along with several aunts and uncles. It was weird to think about him not having any of that. From what I remembered from my initial research on him when I first started at the station, he was an only child, and his dad had moved here from Sweden to play for Detroit. His mom had some athleticism in her life, but I think she'd also been estranged from her family. That meant that Silas was alone, the only one to help his dad deal with the immense grief he must have been going through.

When he reached out and pulled my forehead to his lips, placing a soft kiss there, I felt a knot in my throat. I wanted to go back in time and help that young man, but that wasn't something that could ever be done.

"Thank you," he whispered against me.

"For what?" I asked, not moving.

"Just for being here," he said, pulling me closer to him. "For not asking questions, not demanding to know more. I don't know that I've ever met anyone who hasn't pushed for more specifics. It fucking sucks to think that some people only want the gory details. Especially the ones who want to use them to give themselves a leg up."

"Well," I said, pressing my lips to his chest. "Thank you for being willing to be vulnerable with me. If you want to share more, I'll listen. If you don't, I won't push."

"Where the fuck have you been all my life?" he asked, pulling back to look me in the eyes. I shrugged, not really sure how to answer that question. "I don't know if we can make this work, but I'm willing to try. You make me feel safe."

The last word came out sort of strained, and he pulled me back against his chest. My guess was he didn't want me to see how weak and vulnerable he was in that moment.

CHAPTER TWENTY-SIX

S ilas...

Fixing lunch with Emily beside me was a new experience. Of course, there wasn't much to do, since my meals were prepared by Mrs. Morris, but it was nice to have someone there to share the food with. Someone who actually listened to and, more importantly, heard me when I said things. It was different from anything I'd ever experienced.

My relationship meter had been broken a long time ago, and I never saw myself connecting with anyone on a level where I could feel safe being vulnerable. How this woman had given me that freedom was beyond me. I hadn't set out to be in any kind of situation like this, and yet, here I was, opening up to her about so many things in my past. And she just accepted me as I was, without judgment.

"We should get some more cameras," I said when we were cleaning up from lunch.

"For what?" she asked.

"The interview," I replied, as if it were obvious. "Can't exactly do it all with one phone. Besides, it'll give you a reason to explain the change in your appearance. And mine."

"True," she said. "Kinda hard to say I did it all in one afternoon when I look completely different from how I did when I got here."

"That's because you look well and truly fucked," I said. "It's a good look on you, too. Might have to replicate it again. Several times."

"Maybe after we finish the interview," she said. "But more cameras would be good. It's not like I can grab some from the stadium to use, but phones do a pretty good job in a pinch."

"Well," I said. "I've got mine we can use. You've got yours, which should be charged by now. Didn't you say you had another one?"

"I do," she said. "But it's at my place. I was thinking of running home to change and grab my makeup bag, too. Then, the change of appearance is very clear."

"How are you going to explain it, though?" I asked.

"You invited me to do a tour," she said. "I jumped at it without planning ahead. Once the tour was over, you agreed to a sit-down interview, so I had to get the extra cameras, and figured I'd change while I did that."

"You make it sound so logical," I said. "Like you've done this before."

"No," she said. "This," she added, waving her hand between us, "has never happened before. In fact, it's a rule I've lived by for quite a while."

"I see," I said. "You're a rebel, then. Breaking rules and shit?"

She laughed, a sound I liked a lot, and I decided I needed to make it happen again. Wasn't sure how I was gonna make it happen, but I'd figure it out.

"This is a rule I've never broken," she said. "Never figured I would, either. What is it about you? You make me wanna be bad."

"Bad?" I asked.

"Yeah," she said, color pinking her cheeks. "I don't do shit like this. Hook up with someone on a whim. I mean, in college, sure. But once I graduated, I knew I had to grow up. I've had boyfriends, but none of them really panned out."

"I see," I said. "When did your last relationship end?"

"June," she said. "Dude was a cold fish. Didn't participate in anything. Guy before that was all kinds of insecure and controlling. Nipped that one in the bud right away, kicking him to the curb."

"Remind me to stay on your good side," I said.

We'd finished lunch, cleaned up the dishes, and were just sort of hanging out. I really wanted to take her back upstairs again, but if we were gonna do this interview, we probably should get it going sooner rather than later. I said the same to her, and she nodded, agreeing. Kissing her deeply, I reminded her with my mouth and tongue what waited for her when she got back. Of course, she reminded me of what she was bringing when she did.

Finally, I sent her out the door, closing it behind her. I took a breath, then went upstairs to take an actual shower, rather than just getting her wet to get inside her. I also decided to rub one out to keep myself from sporting a chub when she returned. Maybe it'd be enough to hold me off until we'd finished the interview and I could defile her again.

God, just thinking about her and how responsive she was, got me to and over the edge in barely any time. I might have jumped in a little too soon on this whole thing, but I'd cross that bridge when I came to it. I mean, sure, I'd opened up to her, but it wasn't as deep as I could've gone. I had shit in my past that was dark. Maybe I'd give her those stories after she proved she could be trusted a bit more. But they'd be just for her, nothing she could share.

CHAPTER TWENTY-SEVEN

E mily...
  I hated leaving him, but I needed to take a minute to get myself centered. He was such an intense person, and he knew how to use his body to bring me pleasure. Still, I wasn't sure how long I could stay with him. Not that I didn't want to. It was just, all of this was a bad idea, and I didn't want it to come back and bite me in the ass.

Pulling into the parking lot of my apartment building, I parked in my regular spot, climbing out and locking my car as I turned to go up the stairs. I looked up as I got close to the top step of the first flight and had to stop dead in my tracks.

"About fucking time," Gregory said.

"What are you doing here?" I asked him, completely confused.

"Waiting for you," he said. "Obviously."

"No," I said. "I mean, why are you here?"

"I've given you plenty of time to come to your senses," he said. "It's time for us to get back together."

"That's not happening," I said, moving to go past him.

He grabbed my arm, his fingers biting into my skin as he held me where I was, nearly pushing me down the stairs.

"Let go of me," I said, loud enough to hopefully get the attention of at least one of my neighbors.

"You had your fun," he said, shaking me with the hand on my arm. "I let you get whatever wild hair you had up your ass out of your system. Now it's time to do what you should have done when I asked you to marry me."

"I'm not going anywhere with you," I said, panic building in my chest.

"The fuck you're not," he said, yanking me toward him.

"Fire," I shouted as loud as possible, because I knew people would ignore me shouting "help."

He wrapped the arm that was holding my wrist around my middle, his other hand slapping across my face and covering my mouth. I knew he thought he'd be able to just manhandle me down the stairs, but fuck that shit. If anything, growing up with three older brothers taught me how to fight dirty, because they would never let me go just because I was a girl.

Completely relaxing my body, I let my weight and gravity do their work. I made myself as small as possible on the stairs, praying I wouldn't get hurt when I rolled down the steps. He wasn't prepared for it, and my dropping caused him to career forward. Letting go of my wrist, he tried to brace himself as he went over the top of me and fell down the stairs, hitting his head with a sickening crack before rolling to the bottom and stopping.

I waited, sure he was gonna get up and start screaming at me, but he didn't move. That's when I saw the puddle of blood slowly growing underneath him.

"Shit," I said, pulling my phone out of my purse and dialing 911.

"911, what are you reporting?" the operator asked when he answered.

"A guy tried to kidnap me, but he fell down the stairs and

isn't moving," I said. "There's a pool of blood growing beneath him."

"Let me get you to fire and rescue," he said. "Please hold."

I heard a click, then another, and another person answered.

"911, what are you reporting?" the new woman asked. I repeated my report to her, and she asked, "What's the address?"

I rattled off the address of the building, then added, "We're in the stairwell between the first and second floor."

"Where is the patient located?" she asked.

"He's at the bottom of the staircase," I said. "The stairs are concrete. I think he hit his head."

"Can you tell if he's breathing?" she asked.

"I don't know," I said. "I'm at the top of the stairs. He isn't moving, though, and hasn't since he fell."

"Are you hurt?" she asked.

"I might have a bruise on my wrist where he wrenched me," I said. "But it doesn't hurt."

"Okay," she said. The whole time I'd been talking to her, I could hear her typing away on what I assumed was her keyboard for her computer. "Are you able to move to him? Maybe check his pulse or anything?"

"Yeah," I said, standing up. I walked down the stairs slowly, still unsure whether Gregory would get up. When I got close to the bottom of the staircase, I looked down. "His neck is going the wrong way," I said.

"What do you mean?" she asked.

"Just what I said," I replied. "It looks like his head should be looking one direction, but it's going the other way. Like he's trying to look all the way over his shoulder, almost backward."

I heard sirens in the distance, so I knew they were getting close. I'd also heard a few doors opening behind me, but I'd paid no attention to them. All I could think about was what this was gonna do to my life. The fact that he might be dead suddenly dawned on me, and I sank to the step above me, my heart in my throat.

"Ma'am," the operator said.

"Yeah," I said, swallowing hard.

"It looks like the paramedics and fire truck should be there any minute," she said.

"I can hear them," I said, still just waiting.

"I'll stay on the line until they arrive," she said.

"Okay," I replied just as the fire truck pulled into the parking lot. "Truck is here," I said to let her know.

"You good?" she asked.

"Not at all," I replied. "But thank you for staying on the line with me."

"Sure thing," she said, then disconnected the call.

"Fuck," I mumbled as I saw them coming toward me.

CHAPTER TWENTY-EIGHT

S ilas...

After my shower, I'd dressed, made up the bed, and did a general clean up around the house. I figured we'd do the interview either in the living room or up where the trophies were, so I got both areas ready to go, just in case.

When I felt everything was good, I headed into my office to watch some game film to prepare me for our game with San Jose the next night. They were a tough team, but had been a bit off in their first four games, so maybe we could get another win and keep the winning streak going.

As the afternoon dragged on, I wondered what was keeping Emily. I hadn't asked her where she lived but figured it wasn't too far. Maybe she was farther away than I thought, though. By seven, I decided to send a text to see if I could get an idea of when she'd be back. I waited to see if she'd respond immediately, but nothing came through. In fact, it didn't look like she saw it.

Instead of letting it tie me up in knots, I decided to see what other meals I had, hoping she'd be willing to stay for both dinner and after-dinner activities. Maybe she'd do me the favor of putting on that sexy blue bra she'd worn the night before, and I'd get a chance to see the matching panties. Just thinking about it made me a bit uncomfortable. Yeah, might have to take care of that before we had dinner.

Finding the steak tacos Mrs. Morris had ready to go, I decided to go ahead with that, making sure I had all the toppings to go with them. Once I was sure I was ready, I got plates and such out, along with the pan to cook up the meat. Everything else was chopped, diced and good to go, so I just had to get it out of the fridge and set up the island so we could make them to our liking.

I looked at the clock on the stove. I realized it was close to eight-thirty. Emily should've been back by now, which worried me even more. I pulled my phone out of my back pocket and checked to see if she'd responded to my text, but there was nothing. I called her, but it went right to voicemail.

"Hey," I said. "Just seeing when you're heading this way. I've got tacos for dinner."

I didn't leave my name or phone number. She'd know who it was. Still didn't like that she hadn't responded and didn't answer the call. Maybe she was just playing me, wanting to sleep with me, get enough film to get herself where she wanted to be, and then drop me. But she hadn't seemed like it was her play.

"Fuck," I said, running a hand over my hair that was starting to get long.

Deciding my empty stomach was my biggest issue, I started making the tacos. The sizzling of the meat and the smell of spices helped calm my nerves some. Plating everything on the counter, I was ready to dig in when I heard a knock at my door.

"About fucking time," I mumbled, going to open it.

She looked so small and broken on my doorstep that I couldn't do anything other than pull her to me and hold her as she broke down, sobbing into my shirt. She hadn't changed, was still wearing the same thing she'd left in, and I wondered what the fuck had happened to her while she was gone.

Pulling her into the house, I shut the door behind her and walked her over to the couch, sitting down and settling her on my lap, her head on my shoulder, my arms around her waist. Once she'd finished crying, I sat her up a bit and looked in her eyes.

"What happened?" I asked, and her bottom lip trembled until she pulled it into her mouth. I waited her out because she looked like she was about to fall apart all over again.

"My ex showed up," she said, finally. "He tried to take me with him. Said he'd given me enough time to figure my shit out, and that he was done waiting."

I nodded, not wanting to break her stride but needing more information. If he did something to her, hurt her in any way, I was gonna show him what a real man was capable of, and I had no doubt I could take him. There weren't many men in the league I couldn't take down, so some dumbfuck who wanted to hurt women wasn't gonna be an issue.

"He's dead," she said, and my mouth dropped open. "He grabbed me on the stairs. I let gravity do its job and dropped to the step below him. He lost his balance and went over the top of me, falling down the stairs and breaking his neck. I'm just glad there were cameras that caught the whole fucking thing. Otherwise, I'd still be in custody."

"Oh, baby," I said, pulling her against my chest. "I'm sorry. I tried to call."

"They wouldn't let me have my phone," she said against my neck. "It was the worst thing I'd ever been through."

"You're safe now," I said. "I'll keep you safe."

She let a sob out, choking on it before letting it go and falling apart again. I had no idea how long I held her, sitting there, but once she'd finally stopped crying, I got her to the table, fixed her up some tacos, because tacos fix everything, and made her eat before taking her up to my room and holding her as she fell asleep. Fuck, I had no idea how to fix this, and that was the worst part.

CHAPTER TWENTY-NINE

E mily...

Stretching, I realized I was naked, and that I was pressed against a very warm and hard body. Memories came flooding back to me, and I damn near threw up the tacos he'd fed me. God, how had I ended up in this whole fucking mess? It was one thing to run into an ex and have to make that awkward eye contact and ignore them, but what Gregory tried to do, and then what I'd done, I just...

Moving to get out of the bed, his arms tightened around my waist, pulling me further against him. He pressed his lips to my shoulder, and I could feel his cock against my ass. It didn't feel like it was fully hard, but it was close enough that it made me shiver thinking about how well he used it inside me. So different from anyone else I'd been with.

It was like he excelled at everything he did. He talked me out of my clothes, into his shower, and underneath him in his bed, and I didn't even try to resist. Sure, I made a small effort, but when it came down to it, I knew he would ruin me for anyone else. And fuck if I wasn't right. Trying again, he held me fast, his arm like a vice against my stomach.

"I gotta pee," I whispered quietly in the dark room.

"Come back quick," he mumbled, letting me get to my feet.

Padding into the bathroom, I opened the door just inside it, and as I'd suspected, it was where the toilet was. Shutting the door, I did my business, flushing and waiting until the water had finished running before opening the door and going over to the sink to wash my hands. I startled when I turned to go back to bed because he was standing at the doorway.

"You okay?" he asked.

His voice was rough with sleep and something else I couldn't quite place. Whether it was the fact that I'd been gone for so long or what I went through, I didn't know. The care he showed me last night was so unexpected. He was a conundrum, something that I kinda wanted to unravel, but not sure whether I'd like what I'd find.

"I guess so," I replied, and he visibly relaxed.

Walking up to him, I placed one hand on his chest, the other against his cheek, and I pressed up to kiss him. His arms went around my waist, holding me to him as he returned it in a slow and languid manner that made me want to stay right where I was, never moving again. It was like he was trying to get me out of my head, and it was working.

When he pulled back, he pressed his forehead against mine, his eyes barely visible in the low light of the nightlight in the bathroom. He had a hand on my ass, and the other had come up to my shoulder, stroking his fingers along my skin in this mesmerizing way I couldn't explain.

"What's your plan going forward?" he asked.

"There's gonna be an investigation," I said. "But the cameras clearly show that I simply reacted. He was the aggressor, and I was simply trying to defend myself. They told me it shouldn't take too long but that I needed to stay in town until they completed it."

"Does that mean you're not going to DC with us?"

"I can't," I said. "Fuck, I gotta call the station and let them know what's going on. Mr. Davidson is gonna be pissed and is probably gonna use it as an excuse to fire me."

"The fuck he will," he said, and the passion in his voice was palpable. "Let me call the team and see if we can get something going for you. Maybe connect you with the PR people or something. It'd give you a better chance to finish the interview, and working for the team would mean you wouldn't have to deal with that asshole anymore."

"I'm not gonna let you fight my battles," I said, and I meant it. "Much as I would love for someone to go out on my behalf, I can't have that. Especially right now. You can't get wrapped up in this shit."

"Already am," he replied, holding me tight.

How had I gotten into this situation? Gregory was just the asshole ex, but he had never been violent. Hell, he hadn't been much of anything, really, which was why I'd broken up with him. Had he been hiding this side of himself all along? What did that say about my ability to read people? Because if he was able to fool me, who else was?

"Come on," Silas said. "Let's get you back in bed. I'll pee, then I will remind you of how fucking amazing you are."

I smiled because it was just the distraction I was looking for. Letting him lead me, he settled me under the covers, then went into the little room to take care of nature's calling before coming out, washing his hands, and climbing into the bed beside me.

Pulling me against him, his hands roamed down my body, cupping my ass, lifting my leg up and over his thigh, and skirting down toward my pussy. As his fingers slid through my folds, finding purchase inside me, I sighed, relaxing completely and turning my brain off. I lost myself in his touch, forgetting the bad shit that had happened in the last few days and just letting my body exist under his touch. It was everything I needed.

CHAPTER THIRTY

S ilas...

By the time the sun rose, Emily had become putty in my hands. I played her with the same precision I used on the ice—smooth strokes, fierce determination, and a drive to score goal after goal. In this case, though, it was orgasms I was trying to score, and they were hers, not mine. Leaving her sleeping in my bed, I went into the bathroom, took a shower, then started the bath, wanting to care for her in a way she had obviously never been cared for before.

When she padded in, eyes still glassy, I held her, kissing her soundly, then helped her into the tub. She sighed as she lowered herself, and I went and got what I needed to wash her, to make her feel like she mattered more than just a good fuck. She was a good fuck, but this was more about her emotional and mental state.

If I knew anything about how much a person's mental health played in the rest of their lives, it was that a fucked-up brain could derail everything, making the simplest of mistakes snowball into something so big you couldn't handle it on your own. I didn't want that for her, so I went about making sure that she didn't have to worry about that.

"Join me?" she asked.

"Can't," I said. "I've gotta get to the arena. Morning skate is starting soon. You gonna be okay here on your own?"

"Yeah," she said, but I wasn't sure she believed it.

"I've texted you a code for the door," I said, kissing her temple. "You can come and go as you want. Stay all day, go home, whatever. You need me, call or text, and I'll get back to you as soon as I can. Phones are off during practice and the game, but I'll check it between the two."

"You're too good for me," she said.

"Nah," I replied. "It's the other way around. There's food in the fridge, and towels are in the warmer. Just push the off button before you open it. Get some footage for your story while I'm gone if you want. We can finish up the interview when you're ready."

"Thank you," she said with a sigh. "You have no idea what this means to me."

"I get it," I said. "Call out at the station or go in, whichever one feels better to you. Don't go because you think you have to, though. If you need the day, take it."

"I'm probably gonna try to go in," she said.

"Then I'll see you there," I replied with another kiss. "Now, if I don't get out of here, I'll never make it."

She reached up, putting a hand at the back of my neck, and pulled my lips to hers, kissing me with all the emotions she hadn't figured out how to put into words. I understood them all and was happy she felt comfortable in my home.

Walking into the dressing room, I felt myself letting go of everything outside the walls. Not that I wasn't still keenly aware that she was in my space, but more like I knew she was safe. It felt weird to be so protective of her after such a short time, but I couldn't help it.

Fahn and Silver had this weird vibe going between them. I knew the new guy had lost his place just before the start of the season and that, somehow, Silver had moved him in with him. It was a strange thing, considering Silver was much more of a stand-off guy, but it didn't matter to me. They were playing well on the same line, and whatever was going on was making Silver even better, if that was possible.

Viggy was with the trainer, likely due to the hit he took. A few of the other players were around in various states of getting themselves ready for the morning skate. I found my cubby, texted Emily to let her know I'd made it, but that I'd be out of touch until after practice. Then I shut my phone off, sticking it into the little locking box I had, before pulling my clothes off and starting to change myself.

Getting on the ice after a day off was like coming home. The feel of the ice under my skates, the way my stick clacked against the puck, and the overall feel of being back in what was essentially my office. Not even Doyle could fuck with my mood today. By the time we came off the ice, I had worked up a sweat, and I felt my legs burning in the best way.

Checking my phone after my shower, I saw that Emily had seen the text but hadn't responded. Not wanting to push her or make her feel like she had to answer me, I left it as it was and went to grab some food to power up for the game. San Jose should be on the lookout because my plan was to take out my anger at the guy who had screwed up Emily's life on their team, and I would not hold back.

Walking to the ice for the pre-game warm-up, I spotted Emily with the cameraman who was with her a couple of nights earlier. She looked a little worse for wear, but she'd changed into something similar to what she'd worn before. Her makeup was done, but I could still see the red rims of her eyes, and I wondered whether she'd cried more after I left. She gave me a small smile that didn't quite reach her eyes. My nod was small, just to let her know I saw her, which was the most I could do.

As we slipped onto the ice, following Viggy with his smashing of the puck tower, I felt that peace come over me once again. The ice, the skating, and the camaraderie with my teammates helped me center myself. All seemed to be good as we went through our routine, and when we went back to the bench for the announcements of the starters, it felt like things were back to normal. I'd glide on my personal therapist that was the ice and the game, and when it was all over, I'd go home and hopefully bury myself inside a beautiful woman who was more than willing to satiate my needs.

Lined up on the blue line across from our opponents, we waited as the singer stepped onto the rug they rolled out to keep her from falling on her ass when she was on the ice. The announcer asked the fans to stand, remove their hats, and join in if they wanted. When the music started, the lights dimmed just a bit, putting focus on the flags in the rafters and waving on the screen above the rink. She had a decent enough voice, but I was focused on the men across the midline from me. They were the enemy now, and all my wrath would be aimed at them.

CHAPTER THIRTY-ONE

E mily...

Much as I wanted to just stay in bed and sleep the rest of the day away, I knew I needed to get to the arena and do my job. It wouldn't do for me to just not show up. I'd explain things to my immediate supervisor and see what we could do. Hopefully, he'd be able to make sure I kept my job until all the shit with Gregory blew over. The police seemed to think there really wouldn't be anything, but the fact that they didn't want me to leave meant I couldn't travel with the team, which meant I needed to do things in Austin instead of on the road.

Going home was hard. The bloodstain was still at the bottom of the stairs, and it threw me back to the day before. I took a shower, then did my makeup, trying to cover up the bruises on my face. It didn't work well, but I did my best to at least make them less prominent. I'd already had one from the asshole on the team who grabbed me, but the ones from Gregory were worse. The one around my wrist wasn't something I could cover with makeup, so I decided to wear a scarf tied around it to hide that one.

I'd texted Michael that I needed to talk to him, so he was

waiting when I walked into the press booth. Unfortunately, so was Mr. Davidson, which meant that I was gonna have to deal with him as well. Fuck, I wish there was a way to avoid him for the rest of my time at the station, but he wrote the checks, so I had to play nice. I pulled out my phone and opened the recording app I used, pressing record so I could have everything he said available. For some reason, I knew he was gonna try to fuck shit up.

"Emily," Mr. Davidson said, and the condescending way he said my name put me on edge.

"Mr. Davidson," I replied. "I didn't know you were gonna be here."

"Mike said you wanted to talk to him," he said. "I figured if it was that important that you needed to do it right away, I should probably be here as well."

"It's not that big of a deal," I lied, hoping like hell he'd go away.

"Mike didn't seem to think that," he replied.

I looked to Michael, who absolutely hated being called Mike, to get his take on the whole situation, but he was curiously looking anywhere but at me. That told me he hadn't wanted to tell the big man, but was forced to, which pissed me off even more. Deciding to just bite the bullet, I went ahead and laid everything out.

"I was accosted yesterday," I said. "Outside my home. By an ex of mine. The incident turned violent, and he died."

"You killed someone?" Mr. Davidson asked, his eyes wide.

"No," I replied. "He died. The police are still investigating it, but they've asked that I not leave town until they finish everything up. However, they don't anticipate my being in any trouble. The stairwell had video cameras, so everything was caught on them. It's pretty obvious what happened, and it matches my story, so I should be cleared soon."

"Still," Mr. Davidson said, puffing his chest out for some

odd reason. "If you're in trouble with the police, that's grounds for termination."

"I'm not," I replied, doing my best to stay calm. "It's a formality. That's all."

"Your contract says…"

"Are you terminating me?" I asked, interrupting him.

"Well, you're in trouble with the police," he reiterated. "That is grounds for termination. So, yes, I am."

"I'm going to need that in writing," I said. "So when I speak to my attorney, they can follow up with the wrongful termination suit."

"Attorney?" he asked, his eyes wide.

"Of course," I replied, calm as could be. Inside, I was shitting bricks, but there was no way I'd let him see that part of me. "Email is fine, but I'd prefer to have it on letterhead with your signature. Until then, I assume I am free to go."

"Well, umm," he hummed, stammering around his ineptness. "I guess you can work today, and we'll see what to do after the game."

"You said I was fired," I said. "Are you now taking that back?"

"Mike, my guy," he said, turning to look at him for the first time in the conversation.

"I'm not a party to this," Michael said. "You terminated her, not me."

The shrug and impassive look he had on his face told me I wasn't the only one who was sick of this asshole's shit. It was nice that at least he wasn't on the owner's side, but he could've given me a heads-up before I got there.

"You're not fired," Davidson said when he looked back at me.

"You mean you're hiring me back," I said, trying to pull off the same feel my immediate supervisor had but likely failing. "That means I get to negotiate a new contract."

"No, you don't," he said, his face getting red with anger.

"You fired me," I said. "That means, if you want me to work for you now, you need to hire me back on, and with that comes a new contract."

"But," he said, looking between the two of us.

I had him by the balls, and he knew it. He wasn't a stupid man, but he'd royally fucked himself with this little conversation. How I stayed calm was beyond me. Deciding what I wanted and needed with the new contract was gonna take time to figure out, and it wasn't something I was willing to be hasty on.

"I'm not going to hire you back if I have to change your contract," he said, which was exactly what I wanted him to say.

"Then I'll just go home," I replied. "When you're ready to negotiate, let me know. Until then, please send the termination paperwork to me so I can move forward."

I got up and walked away, holding my head up. He hadn't taken my press badge, and I hadn't offered it. I was gonna go work with Micah for now, not telling anyone I'd been fired. Whatever happened would be dealt with another time. Tonight, I needed to forget the rest of the world and concentrate on something that wasn't the clusterfuck of my life.

CHAPTER THIRTY-TWO

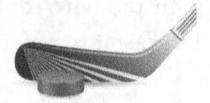

S ilas...

"Yes," I shouted as the final horn sounded at the end of the game.

We'd won, which was the most important thing. Not only that, we'd played as a team, working seamlessly between shifts, each line building on the last, like one well-oiled machine. And it was only the first week of the season. Fuck, even Doyle didn't fuck anything up, which was astonishing.

Everyone was happy, congratulations going all around, and when I walked past the area where the after-game interviews happened, I saw that Emily looked a bit better. I'd have to ask her about it when we got back to my place. That was if she was coming back to mine. We flew out in the morning, and she'd said she wasn't traveling with the team because of the shit that went down the day before, so it was the only time I'd get with her for a few days.

It was just one game away, then one home, then another couple away before we were off to Finland. Shit, I wondered if she was gonna be able to go on that trip. God, everything was fucked up for her, and all I wanted to do was help her out, give her whatever she needed to get to where she wanted.

"Dinner," I said to Keaton when I got to my locker.

"Yeah?" he asked.

"And dessert," I said. "At my place."

"Your place?" he asked. It wasn't our normal go-to, but he'd understood the message I'd given him without going into any more detail.

"Yeah," I replied.

I got out of my shit and headed to the showers, knowing it would be a quick one. I hoped Emily would be down for more than what we'd done so far. She'd been open to everything I'd suggested and seemed like the kind of woman who wasn't afraid to try something new. I just hoped I didn't fuck everything up with what I had planned.

I took a quick shower, dried off, and was in my street clothes in no time. I sent a text to her letting her know I was heading back to my house, asking her to come when she was done, and then I headed out. Traffic was a bitch, but that was because I'd left while most of the fans were still trying to get out of the arena, so it was on me.

I pulled out a couple of dinners and got them in the oven before heading upstairs for a thorough shower before my guests arrived. When I got out, I had a message on my phone from Keaton saying he'd be over once he got ready at his place. That was code for him going all out in his prep for the night. The guy was extra in some ways, but he was a good guy to play with, both on and off the ice.

Going into the closet, I opened the drawer where I kept my toys and looked through them, trying to decide what I wanted to have available for the night. Shaking my head, I opted to grab some basics along with a few of my favorite items that would push Emily. I couldn't wait to watch her respond to each of them. Fuck, I was getting hard just thinking about it.

Spreading the items on the nightstand, I headed down the stairs just as a knock fell on the door. Figuring it was Keaton, I opened it up, only to see Emily there.

"You have a code," I said.

"I didn't want to presume," she said.

"No presumptions," I said, smiling at the suitcase she pulled behind her. "I assume that means you're planning to stay awhile?"

"I hope you don't mind," she said. "When I went home today, it was just…"

She stopped, but I knew what she meant.

"Come here," I said, pulling her to me. Her arms wrapped around my waist, and I kissed the top of her head. "You can stay here for as long as you want. I've gotta leave tomorrow, though," I added. "Away trip, but it's just one game, then we're back for one before being gone again."

"I know," she said, and I'd forgotten she knew the schedule just as well as I did.

"Well," I said, holding her at arm's length. "Stay here whenever you want. Now, let's get that bag upstairs before we eat."

Picking it up, I guided her in front of me toward the stairs so I could watch her ass as she went up. Fuck, that ass was gonna be the death of me. Keaton had a code but never used it unless we planned something. It was the one lie I'd told Emily when I was talking about my place. Keaton had been here several times, but this would be the first time he'd been here for the purpose I had planned for tonight.

"Why don't you go take a shower?" I suggested. "Take your time. I have a surprise for you."

"I can see that," she said, and I followed her sightline to the nightstand. "Is that rope?"

"It is," I said, setting her suitcase near the bathroom. "I wanted to see if I could take your mind off everything that's been going on. Give you a little bit of an escape from the reality that is fucking terrible."

"Thank you," she said, placing her hands on my chest and raising on her toes to kiss me. "It's like you know what I need before I do."

"There's more," I said. "But it'll wait until after your shower. Dinner is about ready to go into the oven, but you have plenty of time. Shower, bath, whatever you want. You don't have to think about anything for the rest of the night."

Her smile was so fucking bright I almost needed to put sunglasses on, and I hoped it would stay like that for the rest of the night because she deserved the absolute best of everything.

CHAPTER THIRTY-THREE

E mily...
    "Shower, bath, whatever you want," he said. "You don't have to think about anything for the rest of the night."

My face hurt because I was smiling so hard. His returning one did things to my stomach that I didn't want to look at too hard. He kissed my forehead, then turned me toward the bathroom and gave my ass a little smack, which made me give a little yip before I went that way.

He hadn't shown me how to turn on the shower, but I was smart enough that I thought I could figure it out. I grabbed a towel from the cupboard he'd pulled the ones from earlier, and shoved it into the warmer, pressing the button to turn it on. Unbuttoning my blouse, I let it slide off my shoulders and drop to the floor. My shoes had been kicked off next to my suitcase, so my slacks slid down and pooled at my feet, where I stepped out of them. My bra and panties joined the pile before I stepped into the shower.

Looking at the panel, I realized it was much easier than I'd anticipated. I pressed the button that had the power symbol on it, then pushed one that read *mode*, and it came up with three options. I pressed the first one and waited. Water came from the showerhead on the ceiling. I pressed another option, and the side of the shower with a row of square black panels began spraying water.

Deciding not to try to tempt fate and end up flooding the whole room, I quit while I was ahead and moved toward the water that was raining from the ceiling, sticking my hand under the water first to make sure it wasn't too warm. Stepping under the spray, I tilted my head back and let the warmth wash the day away.

If only it could wash everything down the drain and give me back my sanity. Gregory had been a mistake, but the fact that he turned out to be so unhinged was not what I expected. Of course, his death decided to screw up everything else in my life, too. Well, everything except whatever it was that was going on between Silas and me. That was something else I hadn't expected.

I looked at the shower wall and saw a shelf that held so many bottles it put my collection to shame. Shampoo and body wash were the only things I expected. He had three bottles of shampoo, five bottles of body wash, a couple of different types of conditioners, and some lotions. The man was a conundrum, that was for sure.

I poured some shampoo from one of the bottles, relishing in the citrus scent that enveloped me when I started massaging it into my curls. Rinsing the suds out, the whole space filled with the scent, and I just breathed it in. I put some conditioner on my hair, winding the long tendrils up on the top of my head to let it do its work while I washed the rest of my body.

Under the shelf, he had a handful of hooks, and from each dangled a different item I could use to scrub my body. There was a long-handled brush, a puff thing, a couple of gloves that looked like they were for exfoliating, and a long thing with hoops on either end, which I assumed you would use to scrub your back.

Opting for the puff, I got it wet and poured some body wash from the bottle with oranges on the label. Slowly, I rubbed it over my body, taking my time to clean everything from the last few days off me. As I reached over my shoulder to get my upper back, I felt a body press against my back.

He took the puff from my hand and continued the process, washing my back in slow and deliberate movements. It was so relaxing having him take care of me. When his hands came around to the front of me, he dipped the scrubber down and between my legs. It didn't stay there long, simply giving a slow cleaning before moving down my legs. He came up the back of my legs, sliding the scrubber up and over the globes of my ass. When his foot pressed on the inside of mine, I let him move them apart, giving over all control to him.

Pressing me forward just a bit, he slid the washing item down to the top of my thighs, then slid them up and between my cheeks, cleaning me there as well. When he pulled it away, I heard it hit the shower floor. He moved away from me, but I didn't move, not wanting to let go of the relaxation I was experiencing. Returning to me, I felt his hand on my body, but I knew he'd put one of the gloves on because the texture was rough.

"Tell me if it's too much," he said from in front of me.

I nodded, and his hand slid down my belly. He slid it between my thighs, running it along my folds, the roughness a new experience for me. There was no urgency to his movements, just a slow and steady sliding along my sex. I wondered whether he would slide a finger inside me with the glove on, and I wasn't sure whether I would stop him if he tried. Instead, he simply washed me thoroughly and then let the glove fall to the floor.

"Let's get you rinsed off," he said.

His voice was rough with what I figured was strain. I could tell he moved away from me because I missed the warmth from his body. Water started to run down my back, coming from different angles, his hands following it to rub my skin. He continued down my back, rinsing my ass, legs, everything, before moving around to the front of me and doing the same thing. When he angled the water straight up toward my pussy, I sucked in a breath, not realizing the rough material from the glove had made me so sensitive.

"You good?" he asked, having shifted the water off my body.

"Yeah," I said. "Just didn't expect it is all."

"Okay," he said.

Raising the water again, this time letting it move up my leg on the way, so I knew it was coming, he rinsed the rest of my skin. When my body was done, he moved me back under the rain from the ceiling, tilting my head back so I could rinse the conditioner. The luxury of having him wash me was something I didn't know I needed, and I knew I would miss it when he was gone.

"I want to take you right now," he said, pressing his lips against my shoulder. "But dinner is ready, and I know you need to eat. Besides, there's a surprise downstairs for you."

He turned the water off, wrapped the warm towel around my shoulders, and rubbed it against my skin. Kissing my forehead, he put the ends of the towel in my hands, then went out and grabbed one of his own. I watched as he dried off and wondered how I'd ended up in such an odd position. Drying the rest of my body off, I headed out of the shower and toward the bedroom, following Silas.

His clothes were on the end of the bed, and he sat down and started getting redressed. I grabbed the handle of my suitcase and wheeled it over to the end of the bed, laying it on the floor so I could open it. I'd made sure to pack some of my sexy underwear, wanting to give him something nice to see when he undressed me.

"Are those for my pleasure?" he asked, and I turned to

look over my shoulder at him with a smile. "I'll take that as a yes."

I nodded, then turned back to my bag. I slid on the deep blue thong, pulling it up over my hips to settle it in place. The bra went over my arms, sliding up to my shoulders before I pulled the bottom of it down under my breasts and clasped it in the back. Grabbing the wrap dress I'd put in the bag, I slid it over my arms. I wrapped it around my body, securing the inside before finishing the wrap with the belt that tied it together.

Normally, I didn't dress up for things like this, but I was feeling a bit extra, and I wanted to do something nice for him. He'd been nothing but kind to me, giving me respite from the insanity that was my life of late, and I wanted to make sure he knew I appreciated it.

"You're beautiful," he said, his hands on my hips.

"Thank you," I replied.

"Let's get you down to the rest of your surprise," he said, taking my hand and walking from the room toward the stairs.

CHAPTER THIRTY-FOUR

Silas...

I'd texted Keaton to let him know Emily was already at my place and to let himself in when he got here. When he walked in the door, I was just pulling dinner from the oven. Coming around the corner, he smiled at me, and I couldn't wait for him to officially meet Emily. I wanted to enjoy her with him, and I wanted her to enjoy both of us.

"Do I know her?" he asked, his voice low.

"You do," I said. "But you might be surprised. She's in the shower right now. I was about to go up and get her. Stay in the kitchen or sit at the table over there until I bring her into the dining room. I don't want her to get skittish when she comes down the stairs."

"You didn't tell her?" he asked.

"I didn't," I replied. "But I don't think it'll be a problem. I've got everything laid out in the bedroom, and she didn't even blink. Adding you won't be a problem."

"Dinner first, though, right?"

"Yeah," I said. "I want her to have plenty of energy."

"We could always start with dessert," he said with a smile.

"I suppose we could," I replied. "As a matter of fact, I'll be right back."

I set dinner on the island, then walked through the dining room to the closet at the bottom of the stairs. Reaching up to the basket on the shelf, I pulled out another bundle of rope, replacing the bin and closing the door again.

"This should work," I said, dropping them on the table.

"I'll get it all set up," he said.

We'd never officially played at my home, but he had been here enough times that we'd discussed the possibility of doing so. My table was purchased specifically so that I could use it for things of a sexual nature. There were hooks and eyes on the underside, far enough in that no one would notice but close enough to the edges to be useful.

"Tonight is going to be so much fun," I said.

"I hope so," he said, sliding the bench away from the table before reaching under to get things set up.

Climbing the stairs, I was glad the shower was still running. That meant I had a little bit of time to get her prepared without letting her know what I was doing. Was it bad that I didn't want her to know Keaton was here until she saw him? Probably. But I didn't think it would be that big of a deal. At least I hoped it wouldn't.

I undressed, leaving my clothes on the end of the bed, then walked into the bathroom, setting another towel out for myself. Her back was to me, her hands running along her shoulder with the scrubber. I slowly pulled it from her hand, and her head went back against my chest, a smile landing on her lips.

Washing her slowly, I made sure to take extra care with the most important bits—her pussy, tits, and ass. All of those would be taken care of repeatedly tonight. Dropping the scrubber on the floor, I grabbed one of the gloves, wanting to see how she reacted to the rough texture.

"Tell me if it's too much," I said as I pressed the glove against her stomach.

She nodded, so I slid it down slowly, letting my fingers run through her folds, pressing just a bit on the bundle of nerves at her apex. Her body shivered, but she didn't protest. Once she was clean, I let the glove fall to the floor.

"Let's get you rinsed off," I said.

I reached over and grabbed the showerhead with the extended hose, turning it on to let the water run down her back. Rubbing her skin, I rinsed the soap from her body, hitting every part of her. When I tipped it up to rinse her pussy, she sucked in a breath.

"You good?" I asked, turning the showerhead so it stopped hitting her.

"Yeah," she said. "Just didn't expect it is all."

"Okay," I said.

I let the water climb her leg slowly so she would be prepared for it when it hit her pussy. She didn't seem to mind it this time, so I continued my job, getting her as clean as possible. Moving her back under the water pouring from the ceiling, I tipped her head back to rinse the conditioner from her hair. She relaxed so much under my hands that I had to work to keep myself in control.

"I want to take you right now," I said as I pressed a kiss to her shoulder. "But dinner is ready, and I know you need to eat. Besides, there's a surprise downstairs for you."

I turned the water off, then pulled the towel from the warmer, wrapping it around her and drying her body. When I got most of her done, I let her finish the task and grabbed a towel for myself. Walking into my room, I sat on the bed and pulled my slacks on while she came over with her suitcase. When she pulled out a sexy dark blue thong and bra, I almost shoved the pants back down to the floor.

"Are those for my pleasure?" I asked. She turned her

head, looking at me over her shoulder, smiling this devilish smile. "I'll take that as a yes."

She nodded, turned around, and pulled the tiny little panties up her legs, the thong sliding between her ass cheeks, allowing her glorious globes to be on display. Her bra went on next, and I almost asked her to leave it off, but I didn't want to make her self-conscious. She pulled out a dress, sliding it around her body like a robe.

"You're beautiful," I said.

I grabbed her hips to keep from tearing the dress from her body.

"Thank you," she replied, a pink blush brightening her cheeks.

"Let's get you down to the rest of your surprise," I said.

Leading her down the stairs, I smiled at the way my table was set. Keaton was a genius in the net, and he knew exactly how to get things prepared for our evening of debauchery.

CHAPTER THIRTY-FIVE

E mily...
        When I stepped off the stairs and looked at the table, I had to pause. The benches had been moved away from the sides and there were ropes that seemed to be connected to the underneath of the tabletop in some way. It wasn't that I wasn't interested in some of the kinkier sides of sex. It's just that I'd never experienced them.

"This is the first part of the surprise," he said, his arm wrapped around my waist, his breath fanning along my ear.

"It looks interesting," I said.

"I hope it looks fun," he said, pressing his lips to the shell of my ear. "But there's more."

"Do you mean the things upstairs?" I asked.

"No," he said.

He walked me around the side of the table, between the bench and the table itself, and pressed against my back, bending me over the table. I went willingly, knowing that he'd done nothing but bring me pleasure every time we were together. His hands slid up my sides, along my arms, angling them up and above my head. Someone grabbed them, and I froze.

"Hey, gorgeous," the other man said.

I looked over at him, tipping my head, angling so I could see his face. It was another one of the players. One I'd seen before but couldn't quite place. He had a warm smile on his face, his brown eyes warm as well. His dark hair was longer than Silas's but still short, and he had enough scruff on his face that it almost could be considered a beard, but not quite.

"Hi," I squeaked out.

"I'm gentle," he said. "I do anything you don't like, you tell me, and I'll stop. My goal is to make you feel as good as possible."

"Okay," I said, my voice small.

"Hey," Silas said, his body along my back, lips right by my ear. "Is this okay? He doesn't have to stay."

"I don't," the other man said.

"I think it's fine," I said.

"How about we eat first?" the man across the table from me said, squeezing my hands before letting them go and standing up.

The fact that I missed his hands told me that I was definitely up for whatever it was Silas had planned. Shifting my hips back and forth, I felt Silas's cock twitch.

"I'm hungry," I said, turning my head to look at him.

"Then let's eat," he said, standing up and pulling me with him. "Keaton, this is Emily. She works for Austin Sports Network."

"Worked," I said, and he looked at me. "The owner fired me today," I added with a shrug.

"But you were working," he said, confusion clear on his face.

"I didn't want to let Micah do everything alone," I said. "Besides, the guy hired me back almost immediately when I said the word attorney."

"Oh, this I gotta hear," Keaton said, turning to walk into the kitchen.

"Come on," Silas said.

DINNER WAS AGAIN DELICIOUS, but I was cautious to not overeat. Nothing says sexy like bodily functions after a meal, and I wanted to be sexy for these guys. God, just the thought of Silas was enough to make me wet, but adding Keaton, who I learned was the goalie for the team, seemed like it turned it up tenfold.

"This was really good," Keaton said. "I think I need to hire Mrs. Morris to make me food, too. You eat like a fucking king."

"Oh, yeah," Silas said. "I'll let her know that I have another player who might want her services in that department."

They grabbed the dishes from the table, including mine, and went into the kitchen to put them in the sink. I finished the wine that was in my glass, not because I needed the liquid courage, but because it was really fucking good. I had no idea how much Silas spent on wine, but whatever it was showed in the flavor.

"Emily?" Keaton said my name as a question.

"That's me," I replied.

"How do you feel about bourbon?"

"To drink?" I asked, wrinkling my nose.

"Yeah," he said, then saw my face. "I'll take that as a no."

"I don't really like any hard alcohol," I said.

"Are you opposed to us drinking it?" Silas asked.

"Knock yourself out," I said, sliding from the stool I'd been sitting on.

Silas opened the freezer, pulled a small bag out, and handed it over to Keaton. I looked at it and wondered what it was because it didn't look like something that should be in a freezer. When Keaton pulled the top open and reached inside, I watched the motion, waiting to see what was hidden within the gray fabric. What came out looked like a rock, and he gently set it into one of the glasses on the island. He did the same thing again, setting another one of the stones into the other glass.

"They keep the bourbon from getting watered down," Silas said, and I looked up at him and saw he was watching me.

"That's actually smart," I said.

Keaton held a hand out to me and I stared at it.

"Your wine glass," he said.

"Oh," I replied, handing it to him.

"Do you want more?"

"No," I said.

I didn't want to muddle my brain any more than what they were gonna do to it once they got to doing whatever it was they were gonna do. My brain already felt like the anticipation was almost too much, so I walked around the island and headed to the dining room.

Looking at the ropes on the table, I picked one up, marveling at how soft it was. It wasn't at all what I expected, and I was thankful that it likely wouldn't bite into my skin when they tied it around me. The shiver that went through me had nothing to do with the temperature and everything to do with the anticipation that had been building through dinner.

Our conversation had been light, more of a getting-to-know-each-other kind of atmosphere. Now, though, I felt the shift toward things that were darker, more carnal in nature. The fact that I wanted to do this, wanted to experience things with these men, and needed to know what they planned for me, made me wonder whether I'd be able to go back to an ordinary kind of relationship.

Fingers ran up my body, lightly along my side, and I didn't know who they belonged to. I also didn't care to find out. Closing my eyes, I let my body feel, just experience the moment. The hand ran down my arm, causing gooseflesh to pebble my skin in its wake. When another one slid up the other side, a shiver ran through me again.

Lips pressed against my neck as the first hand slid around my waist. There was a tug on the tie of the dress, and then it let loose, opening enough that they could reach inside to untie the other side. Whoever was on my left did that part of the undressing, and then they pulled it from my shoulders, leaving me standing in my underwear.

A hand tentatively slid from my shoulders down my back, crossing over the strap for the bra, all the way down to my thong, sliding over that tiny strip of fabric to cup my ass. There were callouses on the hand, and the rough texture reminded me of the glove Silas had used on me in the shower.

Leaning forward, I pressed my hands on the top of the table, my feet already shoulder width apart, which gave whoever it was clear access to me. On the other side, a hand followed a similar path, cupping the other cheek. When they pulled in unison, I wondered whether it was the same person, but it didn't matter. I let my mind shut itself off, making the constant rambling bouncing around my brain go silent.

"God, you're beautiful," Silas said in my left ear.

"Absolutely gorgeous," Keaton said in my right.

Silas cupped my breast in his palm, kneading it firmly, rubbing the lace of my bra against my nipple. The sensation caused it to extend, seeking the friction. Keaton slid his hand over my other breast, pulling on the cup to let it free from the restraint, then pinched the bud, pulling slightly to extend it before rolling it between his fingers. The differing styles were both confusing and exhilarating at the same time.

Kissing down my back, Silas let go of my breast and

moved behind me. Keaton let my ass go and wrapped his arm across my back, his hand moving from my right breast to my left, giving it the same treatment he'd given the first. When Silas pressed my cheeks apart, I relaxed, leaning forward just a bit more. I moved my feet further apart, leaning down onto the table completely. Keaton let me go, pulling his hand from underneath me, and I heard him walking to the other side of the table.

The strap of my thong was moved aside, and Silas pressed his tongue against my clit, flicking it in rapid succession, sending another shudder through my body. When he sucked it into his mouth and set his teeth into it, I clenched, lightning racing through my veins. Keaton grabbed my hands, pulling them across to him and holding me in place as Silas assaulted my pussy. Between his tongue, teeth, and then fingers, I exploded in a rush, my body spasming on the top of the table, waves washing over me in such an exotic flood I melted into a puddle right there, completely drained of any fight that might have been there.

CHAPTER THIRTY-SIX

S ilas...
Her first orgasm was only the beginning because I intended to ensure she had nothing but us to think about while we were away. Sure, she'd have to deal with anything that came up, but if I could keep her mind lost in bliss for the night, she might be up to the fight come morning.

"Come on, baby," I said, helping her onto the table. "Let's get these out of the way so we can show you how amazing you are."

She let me slide her thong down her legs while Keaton unclasped her bra, slipping it down her arms. His care for her was amazing, but I didn't miss the way he looked at her wrist and the bruises there. When he held it in his hand, gingerly turning it over to look at the inside, she sucked in a breath but didn't pull from his hand.

Leaning down, he pressed his lips to her pulse point, softly kissing it. I watched as she held back tears, knowing what it was from and what happened after. I wanted to tell him to stop, or what happened, but I was fascinated by how they interacted. He turned his head to hers, and while I couldn't see what she saw, I saw her reaction. The tears tumbled over her lower lid, skidding down her cheeks, but she didn't look away. Instead, she stared at him, almost as if she were daring him to say something.

He placed her hand down on her lap and stood up, leaning toward her. Hesitating a moment, he must have asked her something with his eyes. I saw her nod, just once, and then he pressed his lips to hers. She looked over his head. The way it was angled gave her a clear shot to me, and I smiled. I never got jealous of Keaton. Any other man would've ended up on the floor, but not him.

Her eyes slid shut, and she leaned into the kiss, her hand coming up to hold the back of his neck, keeping him there until she had taken what she needed. When he pulled back, she sighed, her fingers sliding on her lips as she likely relived the moment. Keaton was a good kisser, so it didn't surprise me she had the reaction she did.

I picked up the strap from the top of the table and started to wrap it softly around her ankle. Making the knot tight enough to hold her where she was but not so tight it would hurt her, I moved to the other side to do the same thing.

"You decide you don't want this," I said, pulling on the rope so she'd look at me. "You just tell me, and we'll take it off."

"Okay," she said.

"In fact," Keaton said, helping her to lie flat on her back. "If we do anything you don't like, we'll stop. Neither of us wants to hurt you. We just want to make you feel good."

"Okay," she said, looking up at him.

He took the task of wrapping her wrists, being careful of the bruised one. Maybe she'd tell him what happened, or maybe she'd keep it to herself. If he asked after we left in the morning, I'd tell him it was bad but that he'd have to get the story directly from her.

When she was secured to the table, I ran a hand up her leg, slowly following its line straight to her center. My fingers caressed the space between her thigh and torso, right where it bent and opened. Keaton had moved to the other side, running a hand down her arm in a similar way, his fingers caressing her breast in a circular manner, getting ever closer to her nipple.

"What would you like us to do?" Keaton asked, leaning down to take her nipple into his mouth.

She moaned, but didn't answer the question.

"I'd say she likes where you've started," I said, leaning down and capturing the other in my mouth.

Her back arched, pressing her breasts into our mouths. I flicked the nipple with my tongue, bringing it to a peak. Not being able to resist, I set my teeth into her, just enough to put pressure on the skin but not to break the surface.

"Oh," she said with a shudder.

Sliding my hand back down her body, I slicked them through her folds, pressing on the bundle of nerves at the top before sliding it down and inside her. She clenched around me, pulsing in time with my thrusts, her breath coming fast and shallow. I popped off her breast and scooted down a bit to get a better angle. Keaton took my place with his hand, working her nipple between his fingers, squeezing and pulling on the bud.

I worked another finger into her pussy, my thumb pressing hard on her clit. She was so wet and warm. I wanted to get more than my fingers in her, but I didn't want to stop the work I was doing. Instead, I climbed up on the end of the table, crawling over her leg to get between her legs.

"I'm gonna eat your pussy," I said, blowing on her sensitive skin. "And I'm gonna slide my finger into your ass."

"Oh, God, yes," she panted, and it was just what I wanted to hear.

Keaton continued to work her breasts as I went to work on her pussy, my tongue taking the place of my finger, fucking her with my tongue, keeping pressure on her clit. My fingers were slick from her pussy, so I pressed them against her back hole, teasing the edges of it but not forcing it in. I knew I needed to prepare her, and the first orgasm likely wasn't enough.

When her body started shuddering, her thighs trying to clench around my head, her arms pulling on the ropes, and her feet doing the same, I pressed harder, just enough to get the tip in, and over the falls she went.

"Oh, oh, oh," she cried.

She flexed her muscles, her head thrashed back and forth, and when her voice rose an octave, I slid my finger in further. Her body went rigid, stiffening up, and she held it for so long that I wondered if she was ever going to come down. Finally, her body sagged, and she let out a rush of air, then relaxed more. I slid my fingers from her and pulled back to look up at her. The expression on her face was pure exhaustion and bliss, and I couldn't help but smile.

"Hey," Keaton said when her eyes blinked open. "You doing okay?"

She nodded, and I watched as she swallowed. I got down from the table and walked closer to her, pushing her hair back from her face. She turned toward me and smiled at me, her eyes hooded.

"You wanna stop?" I asked her.

"Not on your life," she said, her voice scratchy from her screams.

"God, you're fucking amazing," I said, pressing my lips to hers.

She ate at me greedily, pulling her arm to hold me where I was but unable to get it free. Having been the recipient of her kisses, I knew where she wanted me to shift, so I did, and she kept at it.

CHAPTER THIRTY-SEVEN

E mily...
When Silas pulled away from my mouth, I had to gasp to catch my breath. My whole body was sore but in the best way possible. Between him and his teammate, they did absolutely everything to me, and I fucking loved it. When he'd asked if I wanted to stop, I almost cried, thinking he was done with me. His being kind and giving me an out nearly broke my heart.

I'd never been this deep with anyone before, and it was a combination of terrifying and exhilarating all at the same time. I was afraid he'd run off or kick me to the curb when he'd had enough of me, but I was also afraid he'd want me to stick around. Either way, I had to prepare myself for both possibilities.

"You're thinking too hard again," he said, pressing his lips to my forehead.

"Can't help it," I replied, then turned to look at Keaton. "I think you should untie me. I want to run my hands over both your bodies, and I can't do that right now."

Keaton looked over at Silas, then pulled the end of the rope, letting me loose. I wasn't sure I liked the fact that he seemed to be asking permission. Especially since he'd said they'd stop if I wanted them to. But that was a discussion for another day. Right now, I needed to explore these two men so much that I forgot my own name.

While Keaton undid one side, Silas untied the other, and I was free in a matter of moments. I sat up, turning myself to face Silas, my feet dangling from the edge of the table. The fact that I was sitting on the table with my bare ass, I hoped he'd made sure to clean it from whoever the last person was that sat on it.

Thinking about that made me wonder whether he'd told me the truth about bringing women here. I mean, it wasn't my place to tell him who he could and couldn't have in his house, but if he'd had others here, that meant he lied. I couldn't have a liar in my life, and the more I thought about it, the angrier I got.

"Am I the only one you've tied to this table?" I asked him, and he blinked at me.

"Yes," he said. "I bought the table for this house, and I've never brought a woman into it."

"I didn't ask about just women," I said.

"I haven't tied anyone to this table," he said, and I could see he wasn't lying, or at least I hoped that was what I was seeing in his eyes.

"Have you had sex in this house with anyone other than me?" I asked. He looked over my shoulder, then he nodded. "I assume with him."

He nodded again, this time without looking at Keaton. Looking into his eyes, I wondered whether I should continue my questions and why I had so many now. They'd be leaving in the morning, so now was the best time to get answers, but I didn't want to think anymore. I'd done a shit ton of thinking in the last few days, and tonight was supposed to get me out of my head.

"Right," I said, scooting forward on the table. Silas's

hands came to my waist, steadying me as I got to my feet. "This table is hard, and I don't wanna lay on it anymore. We should go to the bedroom."

I didn't wait for them to respond, just turned and headed toward the stairs. They'd either follow me, which I assumed they'd do, or I'd end up alone in bed. Silas had put out several items I might want to try, so if they hung back, they'd lose out on all I intended to do. They were talking, but I couldn't make out what they were saying. My guess was they were discussing the plan of action, but it made no difference to me. I was going to go into the bedroom, pull the blankets down, then climb in and explore.

CHAPTER THIRTY-EIGHT

Silas...

ilthen She took her fine ass out of the dining room and up the stairs, and all I could do was watch. When I looked over at Keaton, he was watching her as well. I'd looked at him to get permission to tell her we'd fucked in the house, but just me looking at him told her exactly that. I felt a bit bad about giving her that information, but I wasn't gonna lie to her anymore. The one was more than enough.

Normally, I wouldn't give a fuck about lying to a woman. Hell, I'd lied to them most of my adult life. Never cared about it, either. But Emily felt different. She wasn't just some bitch I was gonna fuck. Sure, I fucked her, but I wanted her to stick around. If I could get out of my head about relationships, maybe this thing could work.

"We going up?" Keaton asked, his voice low.

"You want to?" I asked.

"I do," he said, finally turning to look at me.

"Sorry about throwing you under the bus," I said.

"No worries," he said. "I figured you'd already told her. Figured that's why you invited me to join in."

"Nah," I said. "We really haven't gotten to past relationships or hookups yet. It's still kinda new."

"You thinking this is more than a hookup?"

"I don't know." I shrugged.

Keaton was the only person alive who knew about my epic failure, aside from the entirety of my U16 team. They all saw how Sarah fucked me over that year. How she came to the rink, asking why I was still there, how come I wasn't taking her out, wasn't buying her shit, didn't put her first. She said hockey was just a stupid game, and the only thing that was gonna happen was that I'd lose some teeth and look like an idiot when I had to get a real job.

My mom caught me in my room in tears, and when I spilled everything that was happening, she hugged me and asked if I wanted her opinion. Then she asked me some questions I hadn't thought to ask myself. Like what happened if I left hockey for her, then she dumped me? Or if I stayed with her and gave up hockey, would I resent her for taking it away? All the things a sixteen-year-old kid didn't think about.

Looking back on it now, I realized I'd put up with entirely too much from Sarah, and I swore I'd never let another woman tie me up like that. I didn't want to end up permanently connected to someone who was only looking for a way to make a name for themselves. Someone who would use me for what I could give them, then fuck off with half my shit.

Sure, Emily wanted an interview, and she went about it by sneaking in where she wasn't supposed to be. But the other night, aside from racing out of my house like her ass was on fire, she hadn't pushed anything I wouldn't want to share. And the walk around my house had been kind of nice. Fuck, every moment I'd shared with her had been nice.

Now, I was standing in my dining room with my best friend, with whom I shared entirely too much with, wondering whether I really wanted to share her with him. It wasn't that I didn't want to share. It's just that I felt like I'd thrown it at her, and she felt obligated to comply. That's not the kind of woman I wanted in my life. I guess I needed to have a conversation with her before we got down to all the good stuff. Something I should've done before bringing Keaton in.

"Can you give me a minute?" I asked.

"Yeah, sure," he said, sitting on the bench next to the table.

"Thanks," I replied, then went up the stairs.

When I walked in, she was sitting at the head of the bed. She'd moved her suitcase over by the bathroom, folded the duvet and top sheet down, and had a towel running down the middle of the bed. There were a handful of condoms on the bed, along with a few of the toys I'd set out to use. I didn't know if she'd tried any of them out, but I doubted it. I guess she was just sitting there, waiting for us to come in.

"Hey," I said.

"Took you long enough," she replied.

"Yeah," I said. "I realized I kinda sprung Keaton on you without having a conversation about it, which is a dick move on my part."

"Not gonna lie, it is," she agreed.

"Which is why he's sitting downstairs," I said. "I don't want to push him on you, or the two of us on you, or any of that. That's a consent thing, and I am all about consent. Do I want him to stay? Absolutely. But if you don't, he will go home. I promise he won't be upset, either."

"But if I want him to stay?" she asked.

"Then I let him know," I replied. "He's just waiting on you."

"Okay," she said.

"As in?" I asked, wanting to be clear about what she meant.

"Tell him to get up here," she said, and I couldn't help but smile. "And you both better get naked, too."

"Yes, ma'am," I said, walking from the room to the top of the stairs.

I looked down and nodded at Keaton, then pulled my shirt over my head. He saw what I was doing, so he pulled his shirt off on the way up the stairs, flipping it over his shoulder before unbuttoning his jeans. I turned and headed back into the room as I slid my jeans down my legs, kicking them off toward the bathroom.

When I turned back to the bed, Emily was sitting on the end, the towel under her ass. I wanted to ask about the towel but didn't want to make her self-conscious. She crooked her finger at me, a mischievous smile on her lips. I wanted to kiss it off her face, but wanted to let her run this show. I'd already pushed her enough for one night.

Keaton came in behind me. I didn't hear him. He was light on his feet, but I could sense him. Her head turned, and her eyes opened wider, the smile growing as she licked her lips. I knew what she was seeing, and I couldn't deny that it was likely a sight she was enticed by. God knew I always was.

Damn, watching her watch him made me want to watch her fuck him, suck him, just do anything with him. He knew how to use his body, and I was thrilled she'd been willing to let him stay.

CHAPTER THIRTY-NINE

Emily...

I was glad Silas let me take the lead. Not that I didn't trust him, I just didn't trust both of them together. They knew each other, had for years, probably. Knowing how the players worked together on the ice, they could either read each other's minds or had some kind of sixth sense they used to know what the other wanted. I didn't like being the odd man out, so to speak.

Seeing them both naked was something else. Their bodies were so fucking strong, with muscles so well-defined. I swear it was like there was absolutely no fat on them at all. Not that it was surprising, considering the work they put in on the ice and in the weight room. They looked like they could have been carved out of marble.

Silas's cock was long and thick, and I'd enjoyed him using it on me because he was very good at it. Keaton, on the other hand, wasn't quite as long but was super thick. I'd never seen anyone that big. Honestly, I kinda wanted to see how much of him I could get in my mouth.

When I turned back to Silas, he was watching me, and I felt a twinge of guilt at drooling over Keaton. Thing was, he was smiling at me with this knowing kinda smile, and I couldn't quite figure it out.

"C'mere," I said to Keaton.

I reached a hand out, grabbing Silas's cock as Keaton got closer. When he was standing next to Silas, I grabbed his as well.

"Mmm," I hummed, licking my lips. "This is gonna be fun."

"We aim to please," Keaton said, his smile matching Silas's.

"I don't know where to start," I confessed.

"What are your limits?" Keaton asked. "What are you *not* willing to do?"

"Oh," I said because I'd never thought about that.

"Let's start listing things," Silas said. "We mention something you don't want to do, you let us know. How's that?"

"Okay, sure," I said.

What I wanted was to take Keaton in my mouth and not worry about all the rest of the shit. But they had a point about setting boundaries. I didn't want to be knee-deep in it and suddenly have them try something I didn't want to do.

"Blowjobs," Keaton said.

"Yup," I replied.

Still holding their cocks, I decided to see how much I could distract them. I began stroking them both from root to tip, grazing my thumb over the head, picking up the precum leaking from them. They were elite athletes who needed to concentrate under extreme conditions, but what I was doing must have been more than what they dealt with on the ice because the pregnant pause lasted longer than I expected.

Not to be deterred, I leaned forward and licked Keaton's cock, my tongue swirling around the tip. He shuddered, so I kept on. When I got my lips around him, I had a moment of fear, wondering if I could even get my jaw to open wide enough for him. Never one to back down from a challenge, I stretched as wide as I could, letting him slip between my lips. My whole mouth was filled with him, and I couldn't get him very far in, but I did my level best.

"That is so fucking sexy," Silas said.

I faltered, nearly gagging on the behemoth that was in my mouth, but I slowed myself down, breathing through my nose and relaxing my jaw a little more to take him further in. When he got close to the back, almost into my throat, I had to pause again, focusing on what I was doing, how I was breathing, and what I wanted. Whether it was a desire to prove I could do it or the want, I didn't know, but he butted the back of my throat, and I swallowed around the tip.

"Oh, fuck," he said just before he spasmed and spilled down my throat.

Choking on both the dick and the amount of cum, I coughed and sputtered. He pulled free, finishing in his hand, some of it dripping to the floor. Thankfully, it wasn't spraying out so much that it hit me in the face. That was something I was not interested in. I knew some people liked it, but I just thought it was gross.

Silas sat on the bed next to me, holding me up as I coughed hard, spit and cum falling from my mouth onto the hardwood floor below me. When I finally caught my breath and didn't feel like I was dying, I wiped my mouth with the back of my hand, only to have Keaton hand me a warm and wet washcloth.

"That was fucking amazing," he said, squatting in front of me. "I don't know the last time anyone has ever taken me that far in. You are a fucking goddess."

"Thanks," I said, wiping my mouth and then my hand. "We should clean this up," I said, moving to stand up.

"Nope," Silas said, dropping the cloth on the floor. "You get a reward for that performance."

I turned my head to look over at him, and he looked giddy.

"What did you have in mind?" I asked, still clearing my throat.

"Returning the favor," he said, looking at Keaton.

"I'm definitely wanting to taste that pussy," he said. "But I have a question."

"Okay," I said, looking at him.

"Do you squirt?"

"Do I what?"

"Squirt," he said. "When you come, do you orgasm so hard that you squirt?"

"I don't think so," I said, turning back to Silas.

"You didn't with me," he said. "That doesn't mean you can't, though."

"I didn't know I was supposed to," I confessed, turning away from Silas to look at my hands.

"Don't be ashamed," Keaton said, tipping my head up to look at him. "Some women don't. Some always do. And some just need the right stimulation to get there."

"You gonna do that for me?" I asked, surprising myself.

"If you want," he said.

He smiled, and it brightened his entire face. As close as he was to me, I got a better look at him. Where Silas was blond with ice-blue eyes, Keaton had darker hair, longer than Silas's, with just a hint of curl. His dark eyes were like melted chocolate with streaks of gold in them. They were mesmerizing, and I could see someone getting completely lost in them.

Nodding, I shifted but was suddenly lifted up, Silas scooping me off the bed and into his arms. Giggling, I threw my arms around his neck as he carried me up the side of the bed. Leaning over, he placed me on the bed and on top of the towel I'd been sitting on at the foot.

"We wondered what the towel was for," he said.

"Sex is messy," I replied, leaning back on the pillows. "I didn't want to end up sleeping in a wet spot."

"Good thinking," he said.

The bed shifted as he crawled up next to me, then shifted again on the other side as Keaton joined us. Moving between my legs, Keaton nudged my knees apart a bit, and I opened for him. It was a little late to be worrying about modesty at that point in the night, considering I'd been naked for close to an hour or more. Besides, I wasn't gonna be able to enjoy his attention if I kept him away.

CHAPTER FORTY

S ilas...

Watching Keaton fuck her mouth was so damn hot I almost came at the sight. I was impressed she'd gotten him in as far as she had, and when she started choking, I worried we'd broken her. Turned out that she was a strong woman and just needed a little air to get right again. We hadn't gotten all the options out, and she hadn't told us anything she wasn't willing to try, but I figured we could ask along the way.

Keaton settled himself between her legs, and she let them fall apart, giving him full access to her amazing pussy. I shifted her up a bit, sliding behind her so she was leaning back against my body. My cock was right at the top of her ass, and it was throbbing, but I didn't need to deal with it now. Seeing how she came apart for my best friend would be another good show. By the time I got off, I would go like a fucking guizer.

Looking down Emily's body at Keaton was one of the best views in the world. His arms were wrapped around her thighs from underneath, his fingers pressing right at the dip where her legs met her torso, and he was buried face-first in her pussy. I slid my arms under hers, and my fingers played with her nipples, sliding across them back and forth. Watching her stomach constrict and spasm as she built to another orgasm, I plucked the buds on her chest, squeezing them between my finger and thumb, pulling to add that pain to the pleasure.

"Oh, God," she cried. "Oh, fuck."

Her legs strained against his hands, but he was a strong fucker, and he wouldn't let her move. I held her tight where she was, too, and between the two of us, she was immobile again.

"Fuck," she cried, her head falling back, mouth open, eyes shut.

"That's it, baby," I cooed.

I watched her fill Keaton's face, squirting like a fucking flood. She stiffened and spasmed in my arms, and I smiled as she just went limp when she was done. Kissing her cheek, I looked up to see Keaton smiling like a fucking lunatic.

Freak, I mouthed to him.

"Holy shit," Emily said, her eyes rolling up to look at me.

"He's good at that," I said.

"I guess," she replied, little shudders going through her.

"I knew you would blow," Keaton said. "You had a look about you. After watching Silas get you off, I wanted to try to beat him."

"What?" she asked. "Like it's a competition?"

"Yeah," I said, kissing her temple. "Everything is. If you're not winning, you're losing. And we don't like to lose."

She laughed at that, shaking her head.

"I swear," she said. "You're just like my brothers with your competitiveness."

"Long as you're not fucking them," I said.

"Ugh, no," she said, making a gagging sound. "That's just disgusting."

"You'd be surprised at how many freaks there are out

there," Keaton said, sitting up and licking his lips. "You're fucking delicious."

"She is," I said.

"So," she said, shifting a bit, her ass sliding along my cock and making it throb. "We never got through the list of options."

"You're right," Keaton said. "Did you want to continue with the list? Or do you just want to try things and stop if it's not what you're into?"

"I was thinking I might like to just try things," she said. "But I'm feeling a bit icky."

"Shower?" I asked.

"Shower sex," Keaton said with a wicked smile.

"If I don't come soon," I said, pulling her ass back against me. "I might be in trouble."

"Oh," she said, then leaned forward. "Why don't we do that before the shower?"

"Come here, gorgeous," Keaton said, taking her arms and pulling her forward, giving me a beautiful view of her ass.

"I wanna fuck that ass," I said, and she looked over her shoulder at me. "Not yet," I added. "We'd need to get you prepped first."

"Let's do it," she said, pressing her chest closer to the mattress.

"She's flexible," Keaton said. "But I think we should get you up on your knees."

Not even resisting, she let her legs flip behind her, pressing so she was up as he'd said, looking over her shoulder at me again.

"That work?" she asked.

"Almost," I said.

Snagging one of the condoms from the bed, as well as the lube and a silicone ass trainer I'd put out, I got up on my knees. I opened the condom and rolled it down my length because I knew once we got going, I didn't want to have to stop or forget. My fingers slid into her pussy, and she was so warm and wet. I pulled them out, sliding the fluids up over her asshole, and she leaned forward more. With a knee, I moved her legs farther apart as I pressed my finger against her opening, it going in just enough for her to feel it.

"Relax," I said, running a hand up her back.

"Look at me," Keaton said. "Big breath in, and when you let it out, bear down a bit. It'll help him get in easier."

"Okay," she said, taking that big breath. When she blew it out, my finger slid in to the first knuckle. "Oh, damn."

"Too much?" I asked.

"No," she said. "Too good."

I chuckled as I worked a second finger into her. She relaxed even more, her breath quickening, and I figured it was time to work in one of the toys. Picking it up, I put a bit of lube on the tip, then pulled my fingers out and slid the toy in with one quick movement.

"Oh," she said, her back arching.

"Let me know if it's too much," I said.

"It's not," she said, her voice breathy.

"Good girl," Keaton said.

Sliding the toy in and out of her in a slow and methodical way, I wanted to dive into her pussy with my dick, but I didn't want to break the rhythm. It wasn't very big, just barely bigger than my finger, but it bumped up with these little bubble things, gradually increasing in size. I knew the pleasure it gave and knew that it took a while to become accustomed to it, but she was pushing back each time I pushed forward.

"Hey," I said, stopping my motion. "I don't want to go too fast, and you're making that kinda hard."

"Then shut up and go faster," she said.

When she turned to look at me, there was a fire in her eyes I hadn't seen before, and it made me want to pound into her myself. Taking her at her word, I shoved the toy all the way in, and her eyes rolled back, her mouth dropping open as she sighed. Pulling it back, I shoved it in again, and her head dropped forward this time. Once more, I pulled it out and slammed it in again.

"Oh, God, yes," she cried. "Again."

Not one to deny her, I repeated the process. Over and over, I pulled the toy back, then slammed it in until she was panting, her back spasming. Keaton looked at me over her and gave me the slightest nod, so the next time I pulled the toy all the way out, lined myself up against her opening and eased in. The noise she made sounded like I'd short-circuited her brain. It was a staccato of the word *oh* and was the nicest sound I'd heard in quite a while.

CHAPTER FORTY-ONE

E mily...

He made the switch from the toy to himself so seamlessly that it took a minute to process. It wasn't that he was so much bigger because he was. The warmth of him inside me just hit differently than the plastic thing he'd been using. Fire stuttered across my skin, and lightning ran through my veins. It was something else.

"Too much?" he asked, and there was a strain in his voice.

"No," I said, shaking my head back and forth. "More."

God, when had I become such a greedy bitch? I wanted all of him, and I didn't like that he was playing it safe and slow. What I wanted was the power I saw when he was on the ice. That undeniable strength the whole league knew he had. He should be using that on me, and here he was, treating me with kid gloves.

Well, fuck that. Taking the lead, I leaned forward a bit as he pulled back, and when he surged forward, I shoved my ass back against him, taking all of him inside me. It was every-thing I knew it would be.

"Yes," I groaned, pulling forward again.

Understanding my need, Silas pulled back as I went

forward, then slammed into me as I moved back. Keaton was in front of me, and I reached a hand out to pull him closer. Leaning in, he pressed his lips to me, but that wasn't what I wanted. With one hand, I reached toward his cock, which had gotten hard again, and pulled on it. I might not have been able to take all of him into my mouth initially, but I was feeling brave and wanted to try again.

Standing up, he leaned forward enough so I could get my lips around him. Maybe if I'd gotten my lips around him before he got hard, I could have gotten more of him in my mouth. That wasn't gonna happen, though, because he was as hard as he'd been the first time. Not willing to consider defeat, I opened wide, and he slid over my tongue.

The sensation of Silas in my ass and Keaton in my mouth was almost too much, but when Silas slowed down, I leaned back, a whine coming out around Keaton's cock.

"I wanted to give you a minute, baby," he said, his hand sliding around my waist to find my clit.

Pushing forward, I took more of Keaton in my mouth. I then leaned back, filling my ass with Silas. The push and pull, forward and back, and Silas working my clit like he had a master's in driving me fucking wild, was everything I needed and sent me flying off the cliff to absolute bliss. Stars burst behind my eyelids, my pussy clenched around nothing at all, and when I felt Silas shudder inside my ass and Keaton pulse in my mouth, the world went sideways. All thought ceased, and all I could do was experience the best orgasm I'd had in entirely too long. The fact that I didn't have to get myself there alone meant everything.

The three of us pulled apart slowly, Keaton holding the edge of the bed until he was out of my mouth, then nearly collapsing next to me. Silas held me up until he'd pulled free, then gently laid me down next to Keaton, and fell beside me on the other side.

"Did I die?" Keaton asked, his voice hoarse.

"I went to heaven," Silas said, and the smile on his lips told me he wasn't lying.

"Wherever we went," I added, my voice rough. "I wanna go there again and again."

"Give us a minute," Silas said with a laugh.

"Not right now," I said. "That might kill me."

"Pretty sure you killed me," Keaton added. "Not mad about it, though."

After a while, Keaton kissed the dip at the top of my ass, then shifted and stood up, walking to the bathroom. I raised my eyes and watched as he walked away. He had a mighty fine ass, I had to admit. When I pulled my eyes back down to Silas, I saw he was doing the same.

"He has a fine ass," he said, and I smiled.

"That he does," I agreed.

Keaton flushed the toilet, went to the sink to wash, and then went into the bathroom. I heard the water turn on in the tub and smiled at the thought of a bath with both of them. Something I also wanted to see was them kiss. Didn't know why, but it sounded hot. They'd said they'd hooked up, so maybe they'd do that for me. I didn't want to fetishize them, though, so asking was gonna be interesting.

"What'cha thinking?" Silas asked, tucking some hair behind my ear.

I bit my lip, not really sure how to ask for what I wanted. He reached out and pulled it out, then pressed his lips to mine, rolling me over onto my back and pressing me into the mattress with his bigger body. All thoughts went out of my mind, and I just existed in his attention. His hand slid down my body, hooking my leg and pressing his cock against my pussy. My hips bucked against him, wanting more than just that little pressure.

"You're a greedy little thing," he said against my lips. "The perfect woman."

"I want more," I said, shifting my hips again.

"Come on," he said, sliding off me and rolling off the bed in one perfect motion.

"If I tried that," I said as I shifted to sitting. "I'd end up on my head or my ass, and not in the best way, either."

"I'm sure it would be adorable," he said.

"Doubt it," I said, standing. "Ooh," I said, realizing I was feeling the action more than I'd anticipated.

"Bath will help," he said.

"Give me a minute," I said, standing still, not wanting to move.

Without warning, he scooped me up, pulling a giggle from me with the action.

"Gotta pee first," he said, setting me on my feet just inside the room with the toilet.

"Thanks," I said, stepping in and sliding the door shut.

Sitting on the toilet, I sighed, letting nature do what needed to be done before wiping and flushing. When I opened the door, Silas was right there, startling me.

"My turn," he said, sliding past me with a hand along my stomach. "Go get in the tub. Keaton will help you."

He pulled the door shut behind him, and I turned toward the tub. I stopped at the sink to wash my hands before turning to the giant tub that was big enough for all three of us and probably a couple more people.

"Come on," Keaton said from next to it. "Test it with your toe first. I don't know how hot you like it."

He held my hand to keep me balanced as I raised my leg and my toe dipped into the water. It was warm but not too hot, so I set my foot all the way down. I wasn't sure how I was gonna get the other foot in without slipping and falling on my ass. As if he read my mind, Keaton kept my hand and held the other as I pulled my other leg up and over the edge.

"Go ahead and sit," he said, still holding my hands to help.

The water lapping around me was soothing, and the scent

of lavender filled my nose, and I sighed again. I could get used to being taken care of like these guys were doing.

CHAPTER FORTY-TWO

Silas...

She had something on her mind, but I wasn't sure what it was. My guess was she wanted to ask for something but didn't know how. Neither Keaton nor I cared about being asked most anything, and if it wasn't something we were into or wanted in the moment, we'd just say so. If I had to put money on it, I'd say she'd never been with anyone who was quite that open before, so she didn't know how we'd react. Keaton was a fucking genius when it came to getting women to open up, so I took my time in the bathroom, hoping he'd figure out what was rumbling around in her head.

I flushed the toilet, walked to the sink to wash my hands, then turned to the tub. Emily was sitting in front of Keaton, his hands on her shoulders, massaging the muscles there. Her eyes were closed, and she looked like she was very relaxed. I didn't want to disturb her, so when I climbed into the tub, I did it at the other end, slipping in as gently as possible.

"Hi," she said without opening her eyes.

"Didn't want to disturb you," I replied, sliding a hand up her leg.

"Keaton has magic hands," she said, her voice low to match the mood.

"He does," I replied.

My hands worked her calf, massaging it as Keaton was doing her shoulder. I could feel her muscles were tight, but she didn't resist or flinch, so I kept at it. Once it felt like all the knots were out, I switched legs and worked the other one. The more we worked her muscles, the more she relaxed. Keaton tipped her head back against his shoulder as he worked down her arms.

"A girl could get used to all this attention," she said.

"We're definitely willing to lavish you with all the attention you can handle," Keaton said.

"Don't tempt me with a good time," she said.

I'd moved closer to them, having worked my way up past her knees. I looked at Keaton, asking without words whether she'd said anything while I was in the John, but he shook his head just the tiniest bit, so I knew she hadn't. Sliding higher, I slipped my finger along her slit, just enough to get a quick intake of air.

"Sore?" I asked.

"No," she said. "Maybe. I don't know."

"Should I stop?"

"No," she said. "Just go slow."

"I can do slow," I replied, pressing my finger against her clit.

Her hum of satisfaction told me there wasn't too much pressure. I kept sliding along her, slipping a finger inside and getting a satisfied sigh in response. Changing position, I got up on my knees to get a better angle. The water sloshing around made her open her eyes.

"Kiss me," she said, and I obliged, pressing my lips to hers.

When she parted her lips, I slid my tongue in, matching the tempo of my finger in her pussy, slow and steady with an even rhythm. I wanted to work her up slowly, build on what we'd already done, and take a gentler approach. The next orgasm she had should be a gentle rolling experience, not the overpowering kind that took her to exhaustion.

Keaton must have stopped working her arms because she grabbed my cock and started stroking me. Pulling back from my mouth, her breathing faster, her hips tried to buck against my hand, but Keaton must have wrapped his arm around her waist because she could barely move.

"Faster?" I asked.

"Yes," she said.

She turned her head toward Keaton, and he took her mouth, his hand sliding up to turn her further toward him. The mewling noise she was making, and the way her hand worked my cock, I didn't know if I'd last, so I stilled her hand with the one that wasn't occupied with her pussy. Yanking away from Keaton's mouth, she moaned, the sound coming from deep inside her.

"Oh, fuck," she said when her body stilled.

"Good?" I asked.

"So good," she said. "I just feel bad that I'm the only one getting off multiple times."

"Watching you is just as good," Keaton said.

"I wanna watch you," she said, then looked down.

"Watch us together?" I asked.

She nodded, but didn't say anything. Pressing a finger under her chin, I raised her head so she was looking at me.

"Do you want us to kiss?" I asked. "Or do you want us to do more?"

Her face grew pink, even in the room's low light, and she shrugged, not committing to anything. I figured she was curious but didn't know how to ask. I didn't want to assume she would be comfortable with anything we did, so I didn't want to start until I was sure.

"Sweetheart," Keaton said in her ear. "We can't do anything until you tell us what you want."

"It feels weird," she said, her brown eyes wide.

"Asking?" I asked.

"Yeah," she said. "I want to watch, but I don't want to make you do anything. It feels like I'm making you be my puppets or something, and it feels wrong."

"I get it," I said. "It'd be like me asking you to do something with Keaton so I could watch. Or him asking you to do something with me. We could refuse, but we'd still know you wanted it."

"Exactly," she said. "If you guys want to, please do. If you don't, I don't want to make you. And now, if you did something, I'd feel like you were only doing it because I asked. God, it's awkward now, and I feel like shit for even saying anything."

She rambled on and on, her words tumbling over each other, and it was kind of adorable. It was weird that she wanted to watch, but it didn't bother me that she'd asked. Honestly, I didn't mind her watching, being an exhibitionist and all. Still, I didn't want to put Keaton in a position to have to perform for her if he wasn't down for it.

Instead of trying to shut her down with words, I kissed her hard, long, and deep. Her hands went up and around my neck, and I pressed my body against her, pinning her between my teammate and myself. She opened her mouth to me, letting me dive inside with my tongue. When I pulled back, I leaned past her shoulder and gave the same treatment to Keaton, kissing him with just as much passion as I'd kissed her. I pulled away from Keaton and looked at her. Her mouth was open and as wide as her eyes.

"That an invitation?" I asked, and she slammed her mouth shut. "Bummer."

"I just…" she stopped, and I could see she was trying to figure out what to say and how to react.

"Was it hot?" Keaton asked.

"It was," she said. "And I feel like I was intruding."

"Nah, baby," I said. "You were right in the middle. Literally."

"Right where you belong," Keaton said. "At least for tonight."

She shivered, and I realized the water had gotten cold.

"Let's get out," I said.

Easing back from them, I got up and out of the tub, grabbed towels for all of us, then helped Emily out of the tub, wrapping her in one of the towels and rubbing it along her body. Keaton got out behind her, taking over the job of getting her dry. Between the two of us, we got her dried off, then he got her set in bed before coming back into the bathroom.

"You good?" I asked.

"Yeah," he said. "You want to do more for her? Or just do her more?"

"What do you wanna do?" I asked.

"Her reaction to the kiss was over the top," he said. "Not sure she's ever seen two guys together. Kinda afraid she'll lose it, though."

"Yeah," I agreed. "Let's focus on her for the night."

"We better get to it, though," he said. "Tomorrow is gonna get here fucking early."

"Yeah," I said.

CHAPTER FORTY-THREE

Emily...

After Keaton put me in bed, he went back to the bathroom. I wondered what they were talking about, but I was too tired to concentrate. I felt them climb into bed and cuddle up with me, but it was a fleeting thing, like a dream coming to life. My body had been worked over in all the best ways, and I drifted off wrapped between them.

"Hey," Silas said as he brushed hair from my face.

"Hey," I said, arching my back in a stretch. "You're dressed."

"Yeah," he said. "We're heading to the stadium to get the bus to the plane. You gonna be good by yourself?"

"Sure," I said. "When are you coming home?"

"Travel today," he said. "Game tomorrow, travel home after that. One game here, two away, then another here before we head to Finland."

"How many days?"

"Just over a week," he said. "I'm gonna be tired and sore. Oh, and Mrs. Morris will be by today or tomorrow. I didn't want you to freak when she came in."

"Should I go home?" I asked, my chest tightening.

"No," he said, kissing my forehead. "She knows you're here, so she will probably ask you what kind of things you want to eat so she can also make meals for you."

"She doesn't have to—"

"She likes to do it," I said.

"Yo, Si, let's go," Keaton shouted from the main floor.

"Gotta go," he said, kissing me. "Text me if you need anything."

"Okay," I said, and he was out the bedroom door.

I heard the door open and close downstairs, then heard the lock close with its chime. And just like that, I was all alone in a big house. First thing I needed to do was pee. After that, I'd figure out the next steps because I wasn't just gonna sit around and do nothing.

Pulling out one of the breakfast meals Silas had in the fridge, I turned on the oven as the instructions indicated, then grabbed a plate and mug from the cupboard, dropping a pod into the coffee maker. Looking around the kitchen, my eyes went through the walkway to the dining room, and I saw the ropes were still on the table, along with the clothes I'd taken off.

"Well," I said, walking over to them. "Guess this'll be where I start."

The oven buzzed, indicating it was at temperature, so I slid the food in, set the timer, and then got to work picking up my clothes and taking them upstairs. Not wanting to leave the oven for long, I figured I'd clean the bedroom after I ate. The coffee was ready when I returned to the kitchen, so I doctored it up, taking a sip of the rich liquid.

It was such a normal morning—making breakfast, although not how I normally did it; cleaning up after myself, and making the bed. Just normal shit everyone did. But some-how, in this space, it felt special. And, me being me, I wanted to make sure that I was the best houseguest I could be. I did try to undo the ropes on the table, but I couldn't figure out the knots, so I left them, not wanting to ruin either the ropes or the table.

I left a note on the counter, telling him I probably wouldn't see him until the next home game. The police had left a message asking me to bring anything that showed I was no longer with Gregory, as well as anything that might indicate why he tried to grab me. It wasn't something I wanted to think about, but I knew it needed to be done.

Much as I wanted to just stay at Silas's house, I knew I needed to go into the station and deal with the firing and rehiring situation. It wasn't gonna sort itself out, and I needed to settle things once and for all on that front. I'd set up a meeting with the union rep to discuss everything at the station before we met with HR. After that, I'd go to my apartment and see if I could find anything that might help the police, although I wasn't sure what they might need. Since it wasn't my first stop, I had time to ponder on it.

I'd downloaded the copy of my contract to my laptop so I'd know what I was talking about when I met with my rep, as well as the recording of the conversation I'd had with the owner. I had emailed a copy to my rep but wanted it to be on my computer as well. I obviously had it backed up in several locations, just so no one could "lose" it by accident.

There wasn't really any kind of protocol when it came to what had happened to me. If I'd been arrested or anything, they likely could've fired me for that, but I hadn't. It was just a case of Mr. Davidson being a dick. And he always was to women. There had been numerous issues with him, but this one felt like it might just make a difference.

Of course, if things went south with the station, maybe I could hook up with that documentary woman. She seemed to know what was going on in the world. If her show did well, I might connect with her and see about doing something in that direction. Everything kind of hinged on the meetings today, though, so I guess I needed to slow down and deal with the immediate issues first.

Driving into the station felt weird, knowing the players, coaches, and that whole entourage were on their way to Washington for their game, but I was left behind. The police hadn't told me how long I had to stay in town, but I didn't figure it'd get cleared up before they flew to Finland, which sucked. I'd been looking forward to that trip, but I guess it wasn't meant to be.

I parked in my regular spot, grabbed my bag, then locked the car before heading inside. The rep was in the lobby, waiting for me, and she smiled as I walked in.

"Good morning," she said.

"Morning," I replied.

"I've asked for a room to use before we meet with HR," she said, turning toward the door.

"Have you been waiting long?" I asked.

"Oh, no," she said. "I've only been here a few minutes."

"I'm glad," I said. "I thought I was on time, but since you had time to set up a room, I thought I might have misunderstood."

"Nope, you're perfect," she said.

Walking through the building, she seemed to know where she was going, so I just followed along. We ducked into an office space that I hadn't noticed before. Closing the door behind me, she sat down next to the desk and pulled out her laptop and a notepad. I took one of the other seats in the room, pulling out my laptop.

"I've got the contract here," she said. "As well as the recording. You're right when you told him you were going to renegotiate your contract. His dismissal was unjust at best and cruel on top of that."

"That's how I felt," I said.

"In your email, you said something about other issues," she said. "Tell me about the last week or so on the job. What things have stood out that were outside of what you normally would be asked to do? And what incidents caused you concern?"

"This is gonna take a while," I said, realizing I needed to think of everything.

"We've got plenty of time," she said. "Trust me, this will be a beneficial meeting for you, and anyone else who works for the station. Especially women."

CHAPTER FORTY-FOUR

Silas...

"That was a fucking awful game," I said, throwing my helmet into the locker.

"Yeah," Keaton agreed as he pulled his gloves off.

Looking around the locker room, it was clear we were all off our game, and that wouldn't do any good if we kept that shit up. Not winning it all was one thing, but being in the fucking basement was not an option. I knew it was early, but we'd been winning. We'd figured it out, and now we were just skating around like a bunch of pansy-ass rookies.

"Everyone needs to step up," Doyle said as he approached my area.

"Starting with you," I barked back.

"Fuck you," he said, turning away.

"Not if my life depended on it," I replied.

He spun around with a comical look on his face. He'd been a dick to Bell from the start, and it was really starting to piss me off. So much so that I'd thought of checking him in a dark parking lot somewhere if given the chance. Fuck, might just chuck him off the fucking bus as we drove to the airport.

"You know what—"

"Shut the fuck up, Doyle," Keaton said.

Dude looked between us, confused, then started taking his gear off to head into the showers. God, the trade deadline couldn't come soon enough, but we were barely two weeks into the season. Hopefully, another team would be stupid enough to take him off our hands by then. The only other way to get rid of him would be for him to do something so bad it would end his career. Not that I wanted something bad to happen to anyone on the team, but maybe he'd get hit by a bus or something.

"You're smiling," Keaton said as he walked past me toward the showers.

"Just imagining a world without Doyle in it," I replied, tugging the rest of my gear off. "And what a world that would be."

The bus to the airport was quiet, which was to be expected. The first loss of the season was always hard to take, but it showed us we needed to step up. Doyle had been right in that we needed to do better, which just pissed me off that much more. The only solace I got was the fact that I'd be heading home to a beautiful woman I could lose myself in, and damn, if that didn't just put me in a better head space.

By the time Keaton dropped me off, though, I was exhausted and just wanted to crash. With as late as it was, Emily was probably asleep already. Climbing the stairs, I dropped my bag just inside the bedroom door, kicked off my shoes, and pulled my clothes off. I didn't need to turn on the lights. It was a routine I'd done forever. When I slid into the bed, though, it was empty. I turned on the bedside lamp, and sure as shit, she wasn't there. In fact, I didn't see anything of hers around.

"Fuck," I muttered, getting back out of the bed.

I went into the room where my gym stuff was, went to the window, and looked out at the driveway. How had I not noticed her car wasn't there? Every fucking worst-case scenario went through my head. She went to the station, and the cops were there to arrest her. Or she came out the door, and the cops wanted to take her downtown. Maybe she'd gone home, and they picked her up there. Or someone close to the dick found her and took her instead.

"Fuck," I said again.

The trains I was trying to get on weren't gonna help me find her, and they weren't gonna help me sleep. I grabbed my phone and called her, hoping she had me set as someone who could break through any do-not-disturb she'd set up on her phone. It went to voicemail, so I hung up and called again, with the same result. I tried a third time, and she picked up.

"Hello?" she mumbled.

"Oh, thank God," I said.

"Silas?" she asked.

"Yeah," I said. "I didn't know where you were."

"Sorry," she said. "I left a note on the kitchen counter. I came home to deal with some stuff, and I just crashed."

"My mind didn't even come up with that as an option," I admitted. "I thought you'd been taken in or kidnapped or something."

"Dramatic," she said.

"True," I agreed. "You're safe though?"

"Yeah," she said.

"Okay," I said. "Sleep well. Will I see you tomorrow?"

"I can't," she said. "I still have shit to take care of. I'll be at the game the day after, though."

"Not sure I can wait that long," I said.

"Sorry," she replied. "This can't wait, so I won't be available. Wish I were. I missed you."

"Same," I said. "Sleep well."

"You, too," she said, then disconnected the call.

Scrubbing a hand down my face, I climbed back in bed, turning off the light to try to get some sleep. It'd only been a couple days since we'd had a fucking amazing night, and it wasn't like I was someone who kept a girl around. I didn't understand my need to know where she was, what she was doing, and missing her as much as I did. I tossed and turned for way too long before I finally crashed.

The morning started the same as any other off day. I got up, answered nature's call, and headed down to make breakfast. Sure as shit, there was the note she'd left.

Silas

I've got stuff I have to do at the station, as well as at home. If I'm not here, I just crashed at home. I probably won't see you until the next game. We can talk after.

E

Short, sweet, and confusing as hell. Doing things at the station made sense, but I didn't know what she needed at her apartment. Maybe she just didn't want to stay here when I was gone, which made me sad. I wanted her here, whether I was here or not. That thought kinda freaked me out for a second. I'd never wanted anyone to stay with me. Fuck, even when my dad came down, I didn't want him staying for long.

"Get your shit together," I told myself with a shake of my head.

I pulled out something for breakfast, noting my fridge was packed again. Mrs. Morris had come by. I got things going, then ate and headed to the training facility. Since I slept like shit, I had only one thing in mind for practice, and that was to fuck someone up. The only person who came to mind was Doyle. He'd been a dick the entire year, and it was just getting started. If it kept up much longer, he'd likely end up getting hit harder by one of us than by another team, which was fine by me.

When I walked into the dressing room, I changed and headed to the weight room. I needed to get that out of the way first, then I could get to the best part of hockey, the ice. On the ice, there was nothing else in the world—just me, my blades, my stick, and the puck. Anyone else was either there to help me with my goal or in my way. There was no other way about it.

"Si," Keaton said as I walked in.

"Hey," I replied.

"You good?" he asked.

"Frustrated," I said.

I wasn't gonna elaborate because there were too many ears around. Keaton knew this, so he didn't push. We would talk later, or not. Didn't matter. I got to work on what I needed to, putting everything I had pent up into the grind. All I could see, though, was Emily, and the things that stood out were the bruises on her body that I hadn't put there. I would never mark her without her permission, and that was what made me stand apart from the other assholes that had been in her life.

Dole walked in as I was walking out, and I shoulder-checked him hard, giving zero shits about how it looked. He knew what he'd done, and I was just there to make sure he never forgot. I'd keep doing it, too, because if anyone needed it, he was the one.

CHAPTER FORTY-FIVE

E mily...
After dealing with the situation at the station and knowing my union rep would get everything worked out, I went to the police station. They'd called to ask me to come in and go through some things with them. When I showed up, I wondered whether I should've contacted an attorney first but was led to an office instead of an interrogation room. Not that I knew what one looked like other than what I'd seen on television or in the movies. It still felt like I was probably fine.

"Thanks for coming," Detective Harris said as he sat with me. "I'm sure this has been a rough time for you."

"I've been doing okay," I said, although that wasn't exactly the truth. I'd actually just been ignoring the giant elephant that'd been sitting on my chest the entire time. "I'm not sure why you wanted me to come in."

"You're not in trouble," he said, which I appreciated. "We just wanted to go over the timeline again with you. Not just of the incident, but of your relationship with the deceased."

"He's an ex," I said. "We broke up six or so months ago, and I hadn't seen him since until he showed up that night."

"Right," he said, as if this hadn't been gone over the last time I'd been in the precinct. "It's just he said something that made us question that."

"What do you mean?" I asked. "Was he not dead?"

"We got some footage from the apartment building," he said. "We saw the incident and know that you didn't do anything wrong. But, leading up to it, he said something to the effect that he'd let you have your fun, but now it was time to go with him. What did he mean by that?"

"I don't know," I said. While I had some inclination of what he'd meant, there was no way to know for sure, especially since he was gone. "It wasn't exactly a nice breakup. He didn't want it to end, but I did. Maybe it had something to do with him feeling entitled to me being with him."

"Your neighbors said you two were pretty explosive," he said, and I felt like he was baiting me.

"We didn't have a very good relationship," I agreed. There was no way I was going to tell this guy anything more than what he asked, and I'd keep it as simple as possible.

"Was there physical violence?" he asked.

"That's hard to say," I said. "He never hit me, but he would restrain me."

"Emotional abuse?" he asked. "Psychological? Financial?"

"Definitely," I said. "Not financial in the traditional sense, but he never liked to pay for anything, so if I wanted us to go out anywhere, I had to take on that burden. We never went out, though."

I didn't want to tell the cop that I couldn't afford to go out because I was paid too little. That was an embarrassment in and of itself, and I wasn't about to share that with anyone.

"Okay," he said. "Who ended it?"

"I did," I said.

"And that was six months ago?"

"About that," I said. "I don't remember the exact date, but it was before the Stanley Cup Playoffs."

"You know sports?" he asked.

"I work for Austin Sports Network," I said.

"Really?" he asked, seeming surprised.

"Yeah," I said. "Have for a few years."

"So you know all the players and coaches?"

"No," I said. "I've set up the interviews for the players and coaches and have met them many times. But my professional life is separate from my personal life."

Or at least it had been up until a week or so ago. Then, they both slammed into each other, head-on, full-tilt, into the boards with no escape. And I didn't even want an escape. Getting lost in Silas and adding Keaton, it was like I'd fallen into some sort of dream space where the rest of the world disappeared. It was only in the light of day that things became complicated.

"We have knowledge that you were at one of the players homes," he said, and I felt the pit in my stomach. "That you stayed overnight."

I waited because I wasn't going to acknowledge something that he seemed like he wanted to use as a threat. What I did when I was not working, and what I did that was not connected to the death of my ex, had no business anywhere near this issue.

"Don't you have anything to say?"

"Didn't know you asked me anything," I said, putting on my best reporter face and not giving anything away.

"So," he said after a minute. "You're not denying that you went to a player's home?"

"What does that have to do with anything?"

"We're just trying to figure out what happened," he said.

"You said you had footage," I replied. "That seems to be the best way to figure out what happened. You said I didn't do anything wrong."

"We want to know what led to Mr. Salizar being at your place that night specifically," he said. "It doesn't appear that he'd been to your place since you broke up, so what brought him back?"

"I would tell you to ask him," I said with a shrug, leaving the rest of the statement off.

"Right," he said.

"Is there anything else you need from me?" I asked because I needed to get the fuck out of there.

"Just that you still need to stay in town," he said.

"I don't have plans to go anywhere right now," I said. "But this is causing an issue with my job, so I'd love to know when I can resume my travel with the team. If I don't work, I don't get paid. If I don't get paid, then I'm going to need to figure out how to pay my rent, buy food, and all the other things I have to do in order to live."

"I'm sorry," he said. "The District Attorney's office hasn't given us a timeline."

"Fine," I said. "Is there someone at their office I can contact to see if I can leave?"

"I'll see if I can get you a number," he said. "Can I call you at the number we used before?"

"Yeah," I said. "If there's nothing else, I'll go."

"Be careful with the players from the team," he said. "Some of them don't have the best reputation if you catch my drift."

"I'll be sure to keep that in mind," I replied before getting up and walking out.

There was no way I'd be going back to Silas's house in the next week, maybe never. Fuck, if they thought I was sleeping with Silas, they could tell the station, and that would fuck everything up. I so did not need this in my life right now.

Walking into my apartment, I shut the door, walked into my bathroom, turned on the water in the tub to mask any noise, then sat on the closed toilet lid and cried. I cried like I hadn't in years. When I broke up with Gregory, I didn't cry. I'd done my grieving long before the end actually came. The last time I cried was when my great-aunt passed away. I'd just started at the station, and she'd been so proud of me. When I told her I got the job, she hugged me like she'd never done before. She'd told me that I'd made the perfect choice and that making sure I never covered my brothers' sports was a smart thing to add to the contract.

That contract had been renewed a couple times since then, but now, with Gregory fucking everything up, like he'd always done, that was in jeopardy. He'd tried to get me to quit when we were together, and now that he's dead, he's haunting me from the great beyond. Just like everything he touched in my life, he was fucking it up. I was just thankful I'd never have to deal with him again.

I turned the water off, got myself up, and headed to the kitchen to make something to eat. It wasn't that I was hungry; it was more that I knew I should eat. Making a sandwich, I sat my ass down in front of my laptop and pulled all the footage I'd taken at Silas's home. If my job at the station was going to go away, at least I'd had a chance to get this footage. I might not get the interview with him, especially if the team put any kind of restriction on that sort of connection, but there was no way I'd throw away what I got.

I might even hand it over to the woman who was following the team this season for her in-depth documentary or whatever it was. Maybe I should talk to her anyway and see if she needed any help with any of that. Sure, she had a whole team of people, but having lived in Austin my entire life and knowing so many of the people within the Aces organization, as well as at the station, she may want to use me as an assistant for her project.

God, I hadn't even been fired, and I was already looking for my next job. Of course, if she knew I was with the local station and had been fired, it wouldn't look too good. But, if I got to her first and got hired on to her project, then I could officially quit and not have to deal with that issue. My heart jumped when my phone rang.

"Hello," I said, not recognizing the number.

"Ms. Jacobs?" the man on the other end asked.

"Who's calling?" I asked.

"My name is Spencer Cotton," he said, and I paled. The last thing I needed was the team owner calling me. "I'm sure you're surprised to hear from me."

"That's an understatement, sir," I said.

"I heard about what happened with you," he said. "That the station owner fired you without cause, and your union rep had come to bat for you."

"Yes, sir," I said, still confused about what the fuck was going on.

"I just want you to know that the team does not feel you were treated fairly," he said. "We heard the recording, which was smart of you to do, by the way. He was out of line at best and so wrong it isn't even funny. The team has asked that he not show up to games in the future and that if he has an issue with one of his employees, especially if it is something that happened at the facility, that he ask us to assist with it in the future."

I waited, not sure where this whole thing was going. It took so long for him to speak again, I wondered if he'd had his say and hung up.

"Needless to say," he finally added. "We think you're doing a great job and feel like you're being underutilized. Once the season is over, or when your contract ends with the station, we would be open to you applying within our media department to see if there's a place you might fit."

"Thank you, sir," I said. "I appreciate the vote of confidence."

"It's well deserved," he said. "The players have told me they respect your work ethic, so that's probably all I would need to know about your personality to recognize that you'd fit right in."

"Again, thank you," I said, still not sure what was happening.

"Great," he said, and I could hear the smile in his voice. "We'll see you at the game tomorrow."

"See you then," I said.

He disconnected the call, and I looked at my phone in confusion. I unlocked it and called the union rep I'd met with earlier to see if she knew what was happening.

"This is Marcy," she said when she answered the phone.

"It's Emily," I said. "Emily Jacobs."

"Oh, hi," she said. "I talked with the station, and you're good to go to the game tomorrow."

"I just talked to the owner of the team," I said.

"I hadn't realized he knew you," she said.

"He doesn't," I said. "Or, at least, I didn't think he knew me."

"What did he say?" she asked.

"That Mr. Davidson won't be at any more games," I said. "And that he wanted me to apply to the team's media department after my contract was up."

"About that," she said, and my heart fell.

"They're really firing me?" I asked, already knowing the answer.

"Not at all," she said, but I knew more was coming. "They were willing to take you back so long as you kept what happened to yourself."

"Did they request an NDA?" I asked because there was no way I was gonna sign that kinda thing.

"What they're asking is that you work the job you originally were hired to do," she said.

"The job I hired on originally?" I asked. "Or the one on this new contract?"

"Originally," she said. "You're supposed to simply follow the cameraman around and do whatever he tells you to do."

"What did you tell them?" I asked.

"I wanted to talk to you first," she said. "I don't think we can do that. It's a breach of contract, and they know it. But I didn't want to raise holy hell if you weren't comfortable with that."

"They want me to go back to being a grunt," I said. "Did they expect me to drop my pay to what I was getting then, too?"

"No," she said. "That wasn't possible at all. But they're effectively firing you without cause."

"Which they can't do, right?" I asked. When she didn't answer immediately, I asked again, "Right?"

"It's sticky," she said. "Your current contract became void when you were fired."

"But—"

"I'm not done," she said, cutting my argument. "The firing was deemed against the contract, so they had to rehire you. That being said, they gave us the option of you going back as a grunt, as you called it, or taking the payout and walking away. I know you want to keep working, but I wasn't sure if you were willing to go back with those terms."

"They can't do that, can they?"

"I've sent the information to our attorney," she said. "I don't know for sure whether it's legal, but until I'm told, I don't have that answer for you. I told them you were returning to the arena for the next game at the role you had before the owner fired you, as a new contract hasn't been signed, and you are under the impression that the firing was illegal and you are still under the current contract. Until we get a firm decision from the attorney, I want you to go under the assumption that the contract you were on when you were fired is the contract you're still working under."

"Okay," I said. "But, just between you and me, should I be looking for another job?"

"My guess is they'll ask us to have you work under the current contract until it ends, then ask that you not return," she said.

"Shit," I said. "Oh, sorry."

"No worries," she said. "Those are my sentiments anyway."

"I guess I better pump up my resume," I said.

"Not a bad idea," she replied. "It's never a good idea to put all your hope in one contract."

"It just sucks that my whole career at the station has boiled down to something that wasn't my fault," I said. "I still don't know how he found out about it."

"That was my question," she said. "I asked them where the information came from, but they said that wasn't the point."

"Bullshit," I said. "God, sorry. I've been around professional athletes for too long."

"Honey," she said, and it had that feel of someone telling you something you should already know but are too stupid to understand. "I understand you're frustrated, and I don't think any of this is of your doing. If I had to guess, someone on staff wants your job or wants to keep you from getting a promotion. Those are the people you need to check with."

"I get along with everyone," I said, racking my brain to see if I could figure out who might have it out for me. "I don't know who might have said something or how they even knew. No one knew what happened, so how would they know to tell anyone?"

"You're gonna have to figure that out," she said. "In the meantime, I've gotta run. You're good to go to the next game and do your regular job. They can't keep you from doing what your current contract says unless they make a formal change. If they do, they're going to be in for a big fight because your contract is rock solid."

"At least there's that," I said. "But for how long?"

"Until they do anything official, you just keep doing your job," she said. "If anyone gives you grief, make sure to make a note of it, and if possible, record it with your phone. If you've got an old phone, you can use to just record your whole day at the stadium, that might not be a bad idea."

"I don't think that'll work," I said. "Sometimes I go into the dressing room, and the men don't always have themselves covered."

"We don't need video," she said. "Audio recording is perfectly fine."

"I might be able to do that," I said, though I wasn't sure.

"Just keep your head up, do your job, and let me handle the rest of it," she said.

"Thank you," I replied.

"Just doing my job," she said.

The call disconnected, and I looked at it and then at my laptop. Nothing felt like it needed to be done, and I was too tired to think about anything more than finishing my sandwich. Maybe I'd take a hot bath and go to bed early. If only life solved itself with a sandwich and a bath.

CHAPTER FORTY-SIX

S ilas...
    I'd sent a text to Emily after practice but hadn't heard back. My guess was she was dealing with the firing the owner of the station did to her. Much as I wanted to get back into her, I knew she likely needed time, so I wasn't gonna push.

"Dinner?" Keaton asked as he sat down next to me.

"Not tonight," I said.

"Cool," he replied as he pulled his gear off.

I'd already changed, so I grabbed my bag and headed home. The drive wasn't long, but the whole way, I felt like someone was following me, and it just pissed me off more. Instead of going home, I went to a grocery store. Not that I needed anything, but I didn't want anyone to follow me to my house.

Climbing out of my car, I checked to make sure it was locked, then went to the back end and put my foot on the bumper, making sure my shoelaces were tied. Really, though, I was looking around to see if anything set off my spidey senses more than what they'd been while I was driving. I noticed a big SUV idling in the lane next to where I was parked, but the windows were too dark to see in it.

Satisfied that I *was* followed, I entered the store to see if I could find an alternate exit or a way to get home without my car. Nothing came to me, so I wandered through the store, pretending to look for things I didn't need. After a bit, I saw him. He'd been at the stadium before, but I wasn't quite sure who he was.

He tried to act casual but was terrible at it. I ignored him, continuing my walk down the aisles. Much as I wanted to confront him, I figured that would be a bad idea, so I kept myself calm, walking and watching. Pulling out my phone, I turned on my camera, aimed it away from me, and then put my earbud in.

"Hey," I said, pretending I was talking to someone on my phone. "No, just at the store."

I talked to no one, let pauses go throughout, and hoped it sounded like one side of a conversation. Meanwhile, I watched what I was filming, ensuring I caught some good video of him as I went through the store. When I felt like I had enough, I said goodbye to my imaginary friend and turned the video off. Now, I just had to figure out who he was and why he was following me.

Not wanting to look like I had come in for nothing, I went to the meat section, hoping to find something that would do me for tonight if I didn't cook something Mrs. Morris had left for me. Looking through the glass counter that displayed several different cuts, I opted to just look and see if the guy came near. While he didn't come right up next to me, he came close enough. I figured I could pass the offer of service to him when the guy behind the counter asked.

"Can I get something for you?" the clerk asked.

"Oh," I said, looking up like he'd surprised me. "I'm still deciding. Go ahead," I said to the guy who'd been following me.

"I, uh, well," he stammered, sounding like he'd been caught where he shouldn't be, which was exactly what I was hoping.

Instead of continuing to sound like a fool, he turned and walked away, not looking back at all.

"That was weird," the guy said.

"He's been following me," I replied. "I've been trying to get him to leave me alone, but he hasn't cooperated."

"Need me to call security?" he asked as he looked me up and down. "Not that you need any help."

"Don't need to be getting into anything here," I said. "If you want to call security, ask them to make sure he leaves the parking lot. That'd be great."

"Won't he just follow you when you leave?"

"Not if I don't drive my own car," I said. Pulling my phone back out, I dialed Keaton, but he didn't answer. As much as I didn't want to bother her, I decided to try Emily. I could've called another of the guys, but I didn't need them having to deal with this shit, too.

"Hello," she said when she answered.

"I know you said you had stuff to do," I said. "And I wouldn't call if I didn't think it was needed."

"What's wrong?" she asked, the concern clear in her voice.

"Someone followed me from the training facility tonight," I said.

"Who?" she asked.

"Don't know," I replied. "I got some video. I've seen him around the stadium, but don't know who he is."

"That's weird," she said.

"Agreed," I said. "You don't want to come pick me up by chance, do you?"

"Now?"

"Or whenever," I said. That's when I heard water sloshing. "Shit, you're in the tub. I'm sorry."

"It's fine," she said. "I needed to get out, anyway."

I'd walked away from the meat counter so the guy behind it didn't overhear my conversation and was now glad for it.

"We can go to dinner," I said. "My treat."

"I really shouldn't be seen out with you," she said, and I didn't like the sound of that. "I mean, until I figure everything out with the station and stuff. I wouldn't want it to look like we were doing anything."

"You still have to finish the interview," I said. "We can plan that at dinner."

"Are you sure you want to do that?" she asked.

"Yeah," I said. "Why wouldn't I?"

"I don't know," she said. "I didn't think you'd want to hang out with the crazy reporter lady anymore."

"Hey," I said, a bit firmer than intended. "You're not crazy."

"My life seems to disagree with that statement," she said.

I could hear material moving, so I assumed she was drying off or getting dressed. God, all I wanted was for her to stay naked and for me to get to her. But with someone following me, I didn't dare lead them to her place.

"I just don't want to chance this guy following me home," I said. "And you might know him. I mean, you're around the stadium all the time, so he might be a familiar face to you."

"Okay," she said. "Where are you?"

I gave her the store's name, then said, "Take your time. I'm not going anywhere."

"Okay," she said. "Should I come in and find you?"

"No," I replied. "Just call or text when you get here, and I'll come out."

"Okay," she said. "See you in a few."

"See you soon," I replied, disconnecting the call.

I walked toward the candy aisle to see if I could find something sweet to give her when she arrived. Not that I expected her to want anything, just something to do to tide me over, but I also wanted to show her I appreciated her willingness to come to my rescue. Shit, I'd never been on this side of a rescue, and it was weird.

There were way too many different kinds of candy, and I had no idea what she'd like. Just as I was about to give up, a woman standing near me cleared her throat. I looked at her, and she smiled.

"I have no idea what to get," I confessed. "I don't know what she likes, don't even know if she likes chocolate."

"Almost all women like chocolate," she said with a knowing smile. "What did you do?"

"What?" I asked.

"I assumed you did something wrong," she said. "Most of the time, that's when my husband gets me chocolate. Either that or for some special occasion. Is it an anniversary for you?"

"No," I said. "She's coming to pick me up, and I'm taking her to dinner. But she's doing me a favor by coming to me instead of me going to her. It's kinda complicated."

"Sounds like it," she said. "Your best bet is to go with something simple, just chocolate without any fillings or anything, unless you know she likes those. This is a good option," she said, pulling a small bag of Dove chocolates off the shelf. "She can have one or two, and the rest won't go bad if she doesn't eat it in one sitting. Besides, they're nice and creamy, one of the best for the price."

"Price isn't that big of a deal," I said. "But simple is a good plan. I wouldn't say she's a simple girl, just that she isn't…" I searched for a word, trying to figure out how to describe her.

"Plain?" the woman offered. "Quiet? Average? Common?"

"Yeah," I said. "None of those are right, either. She's exceptional, actually. A rare thing, especially in the industry that I'm around. It's not that she's complex or a diva or anything like that. She's just one of those rare women who stand out without standing out. Does that make sense?"

"It does," she said. "I think these will be fine. Not too

pretentious, but not so plain as to be your average thing. They're special without going overboard."

"Yeah," I said, realizing she got it. "Thank you. I really appreciate it."

"Are you going to get anything else?" she asked.

"Like?" I asked, drawing the word out.

"Wine?" she suggested.

"With dinner," I said.

"Flowers?"

"Nowhere to put them while we eat at the restaurant," I countered.

"Hmm," she hummed, tapping her fingers on her lips.

If I had to guess, I'd say she was old enough to be my mom but not so old that she'd fall into the grandmother category. My guess was late forties, early fifties at most. But she looked great. I'd never ask her how old she was, nor would I try to guess out loud, but it felt like she was the mom I needed in that minute, and it sort of hit me in the chest.

"Oh, hey," she said, concern creasing her face.

"Sorry," I said. "I just…" I took a pause, trying to contain my emotions. "You kinda remind me of my mom. Or who she might be if she was still here."

"I'm sorry," she said.

"No," I said. "Not in a bad way at all. I just miss her, and this is a prime example of how much I sometimes still need her around."

"Well," she said, a smile on her lips. "I'm glad I could be your mom for a minute."

"I appreciate it," I said.

"Does she like baths?" she asked, and the shift in conversation threw me for a minute.

"Yeah," I said. "She does like them. In fact, I think she was in the bathtub when I called her to come get me."

"Well, then," she said, hooking her hand through my elbow and dragging me down the aisle and around the corner until we ended up on the aisle with all the body washes, shampoos, lotions, and such. "Find a scent she likes," she said, aiming me toward a display of small balls. "They're bath bombs. Fizzy and full of scent, with enough moisturizer in them to make sure her skin is soft when she gets out."

"And they're safe for anyone?" I asked.

"If she takes baths," she said. "She'll love them. Hell, grab a few, then get a little bag and some tissue paper and make it up into a little gift, along with the chocolate."

I looked at her, looked back at the rack on the wall of the aisle, and back to her again.

"Pick those," she said. "What's her favorite color?"

"Blue," I said. "I think. Light blue. Yeah, light blue."

"Pick your bath bombs," she said. "I'll be back with the packaging. Don't run away on me, now."

The teasing in her voice made me wonder if she was helping me or if it was the other way around. I looked at the balls, all covered in cellophane, and tried to figure out what the scents meant. I could sort of smell them through the plastic, so I sniffed and sniffed, but pretty soon, they all smelled the same. I grabbed a few of them, debating on grabbing more, when the woman returned.

"Let's see," she said, holding one of those little baskets they had for shoppers. "Ooh, these are a nice choice."

"Thanks," I said. "It wasn't easy."

"I got some tissue," she said, showing me a package of the stuff with little flowers on the white background. "And this bag should be big enough for everything."

The bag was just one of those paper ones with handles in a light blue that damn near matched the underwear she wore the first night she came to my house. It was the perfect color.

"Let's go get you checked out," she said, taking the stuff from my hands and setting it into the basket. "Then, we can get everything wrapped up."

"You're gonna help me, aren't you?" I asked.

"Of course," she said. "I'm Sue."

"Nice to meet you, Sue," I said, holding my hand out. "I'm Silas."

"What a nice name," she said. "Seems to fit you, too."

"It was my mom's dad's name," I said, realizing everything about the last few minutes had included my mom in some way. Maybe she was watching out for me and sent Sue to help me out.

We went up to the checkout counter, and she preceded me through the lane. The checker rang up my stuff, gave me the total, and I pressed my card against the reader, hearing the chime that said it had registered. She gave me the receipt, as well as everything I'd bought, and Sue and I headed out of the line.

"Okay," she said, stepping over to a couple of chairs against the wall. "Let's get the bag opened first."

She did that, then opened the tissue paper, setting it next to the bag.

"Chocolate in the bottom," she said, then paused. "No, let's put the bath bombs in the bottom. Then we can put a layer of tissue paper in between those and the chocolate. Yeah, that's what we'll do."

I let her work, placing everything into the bag in her own way, then layering the paper between things and finishing with scrunching a couple of sheets to stick out at the top. When she was done, I stood in amazement. From thirty bucks worth of stuff, she created this pretty little gift for my girl.

My girl? That wasn't something I'd thought would come to my mind. When did she become my girl?

"What do you think?" she asked, holding the bag up to me.

"It's perfect," I said. "Thank you."

"You're more than welcome," she said. "Now, go out there, take her to dinner, and knock her socks off."

"Yes, ma'am," I said.

She patted my hand as she handed the gift to me, and I leaned down and kissed her on the cheek. Her hand came up and pressed the kiss into her skin like she didn't want to lose the sensation or something.

"You like hockey?" I asked her.

"Why sure," she said. "I mean, we do have a pretty good team."

I reached into my pocket and pulled out my wallet, sliding one of the cards I had with all the team information, along with the code number someone could use to make sure they were authentically allowed to get tickets.

"I play for the Aces," I said. "It would be my honor to have you come to one of the games this season. If you call the number here," I said, pointing it out. "And give them my name and this number, you can get a ticket reserved in your name."

"You really want me to come to a game?" she asked.

"Of course I do," I said.

"Thank you," she said, her voice a bit shaky.

"You have no idea what this means to me," I said, holding up the bag.

"Well," she said, swiping a tear that must have slipped out against her will. "You just remind me of my son, and I know that if someone were to help him like I've helped you, well, I'd just be very thankful."

"When you call for tickets," I said. "Get as many as you want. I think they'll only let you get ten at a time, but if you need more, just let them know that you're my adoptive mom, and I'll make sure it happens."

"You're so sweet," she said just as my phone buzzed in my pocket.

"I think that's my girl," I said, pulling it out and seeing her name on the screen. "Hey," I said into the phone.

Sue scooted back like she was gonna walk away, but I reached out and grabbed her elbow to keep her there. I held up my finger, a gesture that clearly meant to give me a minute, and she stayed.

"I'm out front," Emily said. "You almost done?"

"I'll be out in a couple minutes," I said.

She disconnected the call, so I shoved the phone back into my pocket.

"You didn't hang up on her, did you?" Sue asked.

"No," I said. "She hung the phone up. I do have to go, but I really want to thank you for your help. If you need anything, you call the stadium and let them know who you are and they'll get a message to me. And I do mean anything at all. You have no idea how much this meant to me. I really needed this, and you came through at just the right time."

"Shucks," she said, waving a hand in front of her face.

"I'm serious," I said. "Thank you."

She was tearing up, and fuck it if I wasn't, too. God, it was like I had my mom back for a minute, and it felt so right I didn't want it to end.

"You better get," she said, giving me a shove toward the door. "Your girl isn't gonna wait forever, now."

I smiled at her, then pulled her in for a hug. She didn't even come up to my armpit; she was so short. She wrapped her arms around my waist and squeezed me back, then let me go and gave me another shove. I waved to her as I headed out the door.

CHAPTER FORTY-SEVEN

Emily...
        I had no idea why Silas had called me and not one of the guys from the team to come get him. I guess I was just a convenience. He promised me dinner, though, and I had only had the sandwich to eat. At the mention of it, my stomach made the decision for me.

Waiting in the loading zone near the entrance to the grocery store where he'd told me he stopped, I watched the front door. When he stepped out, he was holding a gift bag. He turned to look back into the store, gave a wave, then turned toward the parking lot. I flashed my lights at him, and he made his way over to my car. I unlocked the doors just as he stepped next to the passenger side, and he opened it up and slid in.

"Hey," he said. "Thanks for this."

"Sure," I said, putting the car in drive and pulling toward the exit. "Where are we going?"

"Have a preference?" he asked.

"Food," I said, just as my stomach growled.

"I guess we should find somewhere close," he said.

"Maybe," I replied.

"Go left," he said.

He gave me directions, and when we pulled into the parking lot for III Forks, my stomach growled again. Could my body be any more embarrassing? I pulled into a parking spot and shut the car off. While it hadn't taken long to get to the restaurant, it was an awkward silence as we drove, aside from the occasional directions Silas gave me. Now, we were sitting in the parking lot of a fancy restaurant, and he had a gift bag with him.

"This is for you," he said, handing it to me.

"Thanks," I said. "What's it for?"

"An apology," he said. "For pulling you out of your bath and making you come to my rescue."

"Speaking of," I said, looking around the parking lot.

He did the same, taking time to check the lot.

"I don't see him," he said. "Should we go in?"

"You said you had a picture of him," I said.

"Video," he corrected, pulling his phone from his pocket.

When he unlocked it and got to the video, he turned it toward me. I watched the inside of the grocery store and heard him talking.

"Who were you talking to?" I asked.

"No one," he said. "I was pretending to be on the phone so I could take video."

"Smart," I said, looking back at his screen just as I saw Joe Davidson peeking around the end of an aisle. "Shit."

"You know him?"

"Yeah," I said. "He's the owner of the station. The guy who fired me. But why is he following you? Oh, no."

"What?" he asked.

"When I went to the police station this last time," I explained. "They asked me if I went to one of the player's homes. I never answered them, but thought it was odd that they knew. But how did they know it was you?"

"Do you have any air tags or anything like that on you?" he asked. "Even in your purse? Or your car?"

"I don't think so," I said, but I started to freak out.

"Come on," he said, opening his door. "Let's start with food, and while we're here, we can check your purse."

I nodded, grabbed my keys, purse, and phone, and climbed out of the car. I hit the key fob to lock it, and when I turned to walk toward the restaurant, Silas was there. He took my hand and tucked it into his arm, walking me toward the door.

"Welcome in," the young woman at the hostess stand said. "Do you have reservations?"

"No," Silas said. "We were hoping you'd have an opening. Maybe somewhere near the back or in a corner? Somewhere more out of sight."

"Let me check," she said, sliding her fingers across the screen in front of her. "We do have a spot. Follow me."

I let out a sigh, the relief palpable, as we followed her past a few tables toward a section of booths near the back. She set two menus on the table, then turned to us.

"Will this do?" she asked.

"Thank you," Silas said, handing her a bill.

"You don't have to," she said, making to refuse.

"Please," he said. "We do appreciate you finding us a place."

She took the cash and headed back toward the front of the restaurant as Silas slid into the booth next to me. The way it was situated, neither of us could see the front door, which meant that no one could likely see us.

"Purse," he said, and I set it on the table. "Do you mind?"

"Please," I said, knowing there wasn't really anything in it.

He pulled out my wallet and set it in front of me.

"Check in there," he said as he continued to dive through the purse.

I opened it up, pulling each of my cards out, along with my license and insurance cards. There wasn't anything in it that shouldn't be, but I waited, wanting him to make sure. I'd never had an air tag or anything like that, so I had no idea what I was looking for. When he began putting things back into my purse, I slid my wallet in front of him.

"Did you find anything?"

"I don't know what to look for," I said.

"Anything you don't normally have in there?"

"No," I said. "Just my license, credit and debit cards, insurance cards. Nothing weird."

"Okay," he said just as the waiter came by to set a couple glasses of water down in front of us.

"Drinks?" he asked, looking at the wreckage on the table. "Or do you need some more time?"

"Give us like five minutes," Silas said, and the man walked away. "Do you have a jacket you wear regularly? Anything else that is always with you?"

"Just my phone," I said.

"Any location sharing on it?"

"Yeah," I said. "My mom always likes to know where we are."

"Any way he'd have access to that?" he asked.

"I don't think so," I said, but I got very uncomfortable. "I'll turn it off."

"Not yet," he said. "When you first talked to me in the dressing room, didn't you say you were using an app that the station suggested you use?"

"Yeah," I said.

"Which one is it?" he asked. I handed him my phone, pointing out the app I'd used. "Do you have everything you need from it?" he asked. "I mean, is it all uploaded to the cloud or your drive or whatever?"

"Let me see," I said, taking my phone back.

I went to my cloud and checked, and all the videos I'd

done with the app were there. Everything had been saved there. Then I realized that if this was how he was tracking me, if he was, then he probably already saw all the videos.

"What?" Silas asked.

"Do you think he has all the videos already?" I asked.

"Maybe," he said. "But, if we delete this, maybe he won't have access to them."

"God, how could I be so stupid?"

"Hey," he said, tipping my chin so I'd look at him. "There's no reason why you would think this would be a problem. Your employer told you this was the app to use, and it makes sense that you're using it."

"But that first video," I said, feeling my cheeks turn red.

"Hey," he said. "All he had to do was walk into the dressing room, and he'd see a shit ton of cocks on display if that's what he's into."

"If he has the videos," I said, the pit in my stomach growing. "He could do the tour and everything without giving me credit. He could steal that from me."

"He does, and I'll sue his ass," he said, and the anger in his voice was hot. "You good if I delete this?"

"Please," I said. "The sooner it's gone, the better."

"Great," he said, pressing the app and hitting the uninstall button. "Figure out what you want to eat."

"I don't know if I can eat," I said, and my stomach made a liar of me by making itself heard. "Okay, I could eat, but I don't know what."

"You want me to order for you?"

"Yeah," I said. "Can you? I don't know that I can make any decisions right now. My brain isn't braining right."

He cupped his hand behind my neck, pulled me to him, and kissed my forehead. When the waiter came back, he ordered a steak for me with a baked potato on the side with everything on it, then ordered a steak for himself with asparagus as his side. He also ordered a bottle of wine to go with the meal. When the waiter brought the wine back, he poured a healthy glass for both of us, and I drank it down greedily.

"Slow down there," Silas said, his hand on my wrist. "Let's get some food in you before you have more. Don't need you drunk."

I nodded because there really wasn't anything to say to that. Although, getting drunk might make me forget that my boss was likely stalking me.

"Hold up," I said. "If he's tracking me, why was he following you?"

"Good question," he said. "My guess is that he wasn't sure who you were with, so he wanted to follow me home to see if it went to the same place you were."

"But why you?" I asked, still confused.

"Could be from the videos," he said. "That is if he can get them from the app."

"It's gone, right?"

"Yeah," he said. "I looked to see if there were any other tracking apps, but the only one you have doesn't look like he's connected to it. I didn't snoop too much, but it looked like just family on it. You should check it, though. If there's anyone on there you don't know personally, someone who shouldn't be on there, maybe ask the family who they are."

"Okay," I said. "I can do that."

He gave me my phone, and I pulled up the app, looking at all the contacts on it. My three brothers were there, my mom and dad, and my mom's sister and her kids. Nobody I didn't know, thankfully. Still, I had this skeevy feeling like there was something attached to me that he was using to follow me around, and it just grossed me out.

The waiter brought our food, which distracted me nicely. The steak was thick, and the potato looked bigger than my head. There was no way I'd be able to eat all this, and I felt bad that he'd ordered so much.

"Take home what you can't eat," he said as if reading my mind.

"Okay," I said, cutting a slice off the steak and sliding it into my mouth, relishing in the flavor.

"Careful," he said, his voice low. "Someone's gonna think I'm over here fucking you if you keep making those noises."

My eyes popped open, and I stared at him.

"I like the sound, though," he said. "Maybe I can get you to make that sound again later. With a different kind of meat in your mouth."

I stared at him, my mouth wide open in shock. Not that he'd say something like that, but that he'd say it here in this nice restaurant, with people sitting all around us.

"That an invitation?"

I slapped his arm and slammed my mouth shut, but he just chuckled.

"You're cute when you're frustrated," he said, pressing his lips to my temple.

With the words he'd said, I became very self-conscious, making sure I didn't make any noise while I ate. It wasn't easy because the steak was probably the best I'd ever had. Before I realized it, my plate was cleaned, steak and potato completely gone, and I stared at it in disbelief.

"I guess you were hungry," he said, sliding his plate away from him. "Dessert?"

"I probably shouldn't," I said, not wanting to look like a pig and not wanting him to pay for anything else.

"Bullshit," he said. "You're having dessert."

Looking at him, I could tell there was no arguing. He had the same look he got when he was on the ice going after someone who'd hit one of his guys. That determination fit him, and it was a fucking sexy look.

"Dessert?" the waiter asked when he picked up our plates.

"Yes," Silas said.

"Menu is there," he said, pointing to the small book that

was sitting on the table. "I'll be back in a few, but take your time."

Silas grabbed the book, opened it to the back where the desserts were, and slid his finger along the options they had. He shook his head, then slid it over to me. I did the same, but nothing sounded good. Either that, or I was hoping for something else for dessert. Or someone.

"Nothing?" he asked when I closed the book.

"Nah," I said.

"I'm sure I have something at home," he said.

When the waiter returned, Silas asked for the check. The waiter had it with him and Silas handed over his card.

"My place or yours?" he asked.

"What about your car?" I asked.

"I'll get someone to pick it up," he said. "We've got guys who do that kind of thing."

"Really?" I asked.

"Sure," he said with a shrug. "I just like to drive."

"Ah," I said. "It's the control you like, isn't it?"

"I do like control," he said.

The waiter came back, Silas signed the check, and we slid out of the booth. My heart started racing when he stopped in front of me, his hand behind him holding me where I was.

"Well, well, well," Mr. Davidson said, and the slime from his voice made me wish I hadn't eaten so much. "I see you're slumming it with a lowly reporter. I thought you didn't like them."

"I have no idea what you're talking about," Silas said.

"Not that it's any of my business," he said.

"It's not," Silas replied.

"I'm just saying," Davidson said. "She's used up. Won't be going anywhere in this town or anywhere else when I've finished with her."

"Not quite sure what that means," Silas said. "But if you're trying to threaten her, you best stop right there."

"It's not a threat," he said, and a cold shiver went up my spine. "It's a promise. You hear that, you little bitch. You think you can fuck the players and still work in this industry? You've got another thing coming. There is nowhere you can go that I can't find you. Hell, I'll be ruining your reputation in the entire sports world."

"You done?" Silas asked, his voice icy.

"Not that it matters to you," he said.

"Oh, it does," Silas replied. "You see, I don't like men who threaten women. It's one of the things I refuse to allow anywhere around me. So much so that I'll be having a conversation with the team's owner, asking him to make sure you're never around another woman again."

"Like you could," Davidson said with a cold laugh.

"You don't have to believe me," Silas said.

"Good, 'cause I don't."

"Then get the fuck out of my way," Silas said. The words were so low I barely heard them but I didn't miss the threat that was weaved between them. "Or you can try my patience and see where it lands you."

I still couldn't see my boss, but I could hear the heavy breathing coming from around Silas. The man between us was dangerous on the ice, but I had a feeling he was even more so off it.

"Fuck you," Davidson said, and I heard his movement as he walked away.

Silas didn't move for a couple minutes. I wondered if he was waiting to see if he came back, or if he was counting backward from a hundred to try to calm himself. Neither of those things would surprise me. Finally, he heaved a sigh and turned around, placing his hands on my upper arms.

"You okay?" he asked, his voice low and calm.

I nodded, not trusting my voice.

"I'm ordering an Uber," he said. "We'll put everything you have in your trunk except your key, and we'll have the driver take us to the practice facility so we can hand the guys there both of our keys. I'll have them bring the cars back there. Then we'll go to Keaton's."

"Will he be okay with that?" I asked.

"He will," he said, kissing my forehead. "He has lots of guest rooms and doesn't mind company."

The way he was taking care of me made me warm all over, even after the chill I'd gotten from Mr. Davidson's threats. Fuck, just thinking about them made me shiver. Silas pulled me to him, wrapping me in his strong arms and running a hand up and down my back. He maneuvered us to the front of the restaurant, sat me on the bench that was up there, and then went up to the hostess stand. He returned, his hand out, and I handed him my purse, my phone already off and stuck inside it. His hand slipped along my cheek, a reassurance that he was there, before handing my purse to the hostess with my keys.

"She'll put them in the trunk," he said. "The Uber is on the way, and we'll have him drive us around the city for a while before heading to the facility."

"Thank you," I said.

"Oh, shit," he said, opening the door to the parking lot. "Grab the bag in the front seat, would you?"

He waited a minute, I assumed for her response, and then came back in, sitting next to me. Wrapping his arm around my shoulders, he pulled me against him as we waited for the car service to come and pick us up. I tried to figure out how my life had become so complicated in such a short amount of time.

CHAPTER FORTY-EIGHT

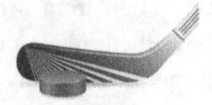

Silas...

The driver looked confused when I told him to just drive around, didn't matter where, and to make several turns, going back the same way we came, over and over. I handed him a couple hundreds as we got in to smooth the concern from his face, and he smiled and did as he was told. Holding Emily in the back seat, we watched as the city went by, the downtown area, some of the nicer neighborhoods, then back to the city before heading out toward the airport, which was a fucking brilliant idea, and then back to the downtown area. Finally, after we'd been going nowhere fast, he headed to the practice facility. I hopped out of the car and headed toward the security shack near the entrance.

"Hey," Arthur, one of the security guys, said as I walked up to him.

"Anyone around that can go pick up a couple cars?" I asked.

"Sure," he said. "May take a bit, but if you can wait."

"Don't need them until tomorrow," I said. "Just have them brought back here. If there's a spot they can stay inside, that'd be better."

"Can do," he said.

I handed him the keys, told him where they were, and then headed back to the Uber.

"Okay," I said to Emily. "Ready to go to Keaton's?"

"You sure we should?"

"I can call him," I said.

"I don't want him to be stuck in this situation, too," she said.

"Hotel?" I asked, and she nodded. "Give me a minute, and I'll let you know where we're going."

"No problem," the driver said.

I could afford any hotel in the area, but I had the feeling the dick might be watching for her to rock up on one of the higher-end ones downtown. Besides that, I wanted to give her a little bit of an experience, take her mind off everything.

"You know the Commodore?" I asked the driver.

"I do," he said. "The one on Red River?"

"That's the one," I said.

"On it," he said. "You want detours along the way?"

"Sure," I said.

"Silas," she said, her voice low.

"Hey," I said. "Let me do this for you."

"I don't want you paying my way," she said. "You shouldn't have to pay for my mistakes."

"You didn't make mistakes," I said. "You were just unfortunate enough to be hired by an asshole. Speaking of, I need to send an email."

"Okay," she said, leaning her head on my shoulder.

I typed out an email to the owner, letting him know exactly what had happened tonight and what I suspected had happened this week, too. I didn't think Davidson had anything to do with her ex coming back, but I wouldn't put it past him, so I mentioned it, too.

Looking up after everything got sent, I could tell we were getting close. I turned to Emily to let her know, but her eyes were closed, and her breathing was steady. Damn, the day must have been rough on her. I felt bad that she'd had to deal with all that, but I hoped to make the rest of the night better for her. The Uber parked next to the front door, and I unbuckled myself, then Emily. When I shifted to get out, she nearly fell onto the seat.

"Shh," I said, sliding an arm under her knees, the other going behind her back, and I scooped her up into my arms. The driver was out of the car, holding the door to the lobby open for me as I walked in. "Thanks, man," I said to him. "Tip is incoming."

"No need," he said, patting his pocket.

"Still happening," I said.

He smiled, handed me the little bag and then left the lobby. I walked up to the concierge.

"Reservation?" he asked.

"Yeah," I said.

Emily stirred, looked up at me, and then around at where we were, her eyes going wide.

"Put me down," she said.

"Yes, ma'am," I said, doing as I was told and standing her on her feet next to me.

I pulled my wallet out, handing over my license and credit card to the man behind the desk. He clicked on his keyboard a few times, then pulled out a couple of key cards, sliding them into the machine on the desk before tucking them into the little sleeve.

"Room two twelve," he said. "Elevator is there." He pointed. "Breakfast is served from six to ten, and room service is available from the restaurant anytime. Enjoy your stay."

"We will," I said, taking the key cards from him.

Steering Emily toward the elevator, she had her eyes wide open, looking around the opulence of the place. When the doors opened, she stepped in, and I followed, pressing the number two on the panel. I figured there was no way anyone would think to look here for her or me, and I hoped it would be somewhere she could stay until she figured everything out.

The doors opened on the second floor, and I stepped out, looking at the sign across from the opening to see which direction I should take us. We turned left, walking down the hall just a bit before I saw the sign for our room. I used the card, opening the door for her, and she walked in. I flipped the lights on, then shut and locked the door, flipping the extra latch as a safety precaution.

"This is a lot," she said.

"It's safe," I replied.

"I can take care of myself," she said, and I just looked at her.

"It's not about you taking care of yourself," I said. "It's about me feeling like I'm helping. I know you're a kick-ass woman who can stand up against any foe, but I want to play the hero right now. This is just a way for me to feel like I'm doing something."

She shook her head but smiled.

"If you need anything," I said. "We can worry about that tomorrow. Tonight, the only thing you need to do is take a bath, then sleep."

"Really?" she asked. "No sex?"

"I'm not gonna make you do anything you don't want to do," I said.

She put her hand on my chest, raised up on her toes, and pressed her lips to mine. My arms snaked around her waist as hers twined behind my neck, her fingers threading into my hair. She opened her mouth, deepening the kiss by tracing her tongue along the seam of my lips. Allowing her to take charge, I opened, and she slid inside. The more we kissed, the more noises she made. What started as small mewls turned into deeper moans, and she lifted her leg, hooking it over my hip. I helped her out, my hand going under her ass to tilt her pelvis toward me, grinding my cock against her center.

"Too many clothes," she gasped as she pulled away from the kiss.

Not wanting to waste the opportunity, I let her go and began to undress, but she was having none of that. She shoved my hands out of the way, yanked my shirt up and over my head, throwing it behind her before getting to work on my belt and jeans. They dropped to the floor, and she went with them, opening her mouth and taking me in, her tongue swirling around the top, driving me mad.

I reached out, trying to find something to keep myself steady, but we were in the middle of the room, with no walls or furniture around for me to grab hold of. My feet were effectively cuffed with my pants around my ankles, and if I lost any kind of balance, I'd topple over like a drunk. Emily didn't seem to care, though, as she kept up her steady rhythm, sucking me into the back of her throat and swallowing around my head.

"Baby," I said, trying to pull away, but her arms wrapped around my thighs, refusing to let me move. "I don't wanna fall over."

"Don't care," she said after popping off my cock, only to take me in again.

She was fucking amazing the way she gave head, and it was all I could do to stay upright. The tightening in my balls and the tingling at the base of my spine told me I was close.

"I'm close," I said, hoping she'd give me some relief, but she didn't stop. "Oh, fuck," I cried, my hands on her shoulders. "God fucking damn."

I lost all control, shooting my load down her throat as she swallowed around me, causing me to spasm even more. I tried to hold on, to stay standing, but I couldn't move my feet apart enough to maintain my balance.

"Shit," I said, tilting off to the side. "Shit, fuck."

I fell, not hard, but hard enough, and she came with me, letting me out of her mouth just as I landed.

"You okay?" I asked, but she was laughing. "What the fuck is so funny?"

"You are," she said. "You lose the least bit of control, and you freak out."

"I didn't want to fall on top of you," I said, shifting so I was sitting. "I was trying to keep from hurting you."

"All you had to do was stand there," she said, still laughing at me. "I needed that, though."

"You needed to suck me?" I asked.

"Well, that, too," she said. "No, I needed a laugh."

"Happy I could oblige," I said.

I kicked off my shoes, then shoved my pants off with them. When I was naked, I leaned over and pinned her to the floor. Not my ideal place to be in a hotel, but it would do for a minute. My thighs were around hers, so I was sitting on her pelvis, and my hands were on her shoulders, holding her down.

"My turn," I said before standing up and pulling her with me.

I yanked her shirt over her head, her tank top coming with it, then I reached around and unclasped her bra, pulling it off as well. I got to her pants before she could, undoing the button and zipper and shoving them down. Then, I picked her up and tossed her onto the bed, getting a yelp from her as she landed.

Grabbing her ankles, I yanked her to the end of the bed, pressing her knees apart so her legs had that butterfly look to them. She was already wet, and the way her hips flexed upward told me she was more than ready for anything I was bringing. Much as I wanted to just dive in, I wanted to bring her up, edge her for a bit, and then let her back down before repeating the process. She'd been quick, but I wanted to go slow. I wanted the build-up to be overwhelming, and when she crashed, I wanted it to be epic.

Leaning down, I swiped my tongue along the joint where her leg met her body, that crack beside her pussy. The way her hands went to my head, trying to move me over, was comical.

"Ah, ah," I said. "I'm in charge now."

She let out a big sigh but pulled her hands from my head and fisted them in the covers on the bed. It didn't stop her hips from trying to shift so I was at her center, but my hands on them stilled her, pressing her into the mattress. She was everything I wanted and didn't even know I could have, and the thought of someone hunting her, hurting her, just pissed me off.

Channeling that anger, I slid my tongue along her crease, from slit to clit, pressing hard on the nub of nerve endings at the apex of her sex. The shiver told me I was doing it right, so I did it again and then again. When I sucked her into my mouth, the moan she gave told me she was close, so I backed off a bit.

"Tease," she said.

"You know it," I replied, and she huffed.

Realizing that having her pants around her ankles wasn't conducive to my comfort, I pulled her shoes off, then her pants and panties, dropping everything to the floor. Then I raised her feet, spreading her wide and giving me even better access to her most intimate parts.

"God," I said in a rush of air. "You are fucking gorgeous."

The smile she gave me said more than any words she could have uttered. Kneeling on the floor, I held her legs up and out, licking her again and again. When her breath started to come faster, I slowed down again and couldn't help but chuckle as she grunted her discontent. Lowering one of her legs onto my shoulder, I used my finger to rub against her crease, up and down, despite her shifting her hips to try to get it to slide inside.

"Stop," I said, looking up at her. She stilled, but her eyes were wide. "Good girl."

The two words settled whatever fear she had in her eyes, and I saw the desire flooding into them. Looked like I'd found her trigger and what cured the fear, all in short order. I filed that away, determined to use it as much as I could in the future. For the here and now, though, I went back to work, finally sliding my finger inside her. She rewarded me with a sigh so heavy I could feel it all the way to my cock.

CHAPTER FORTY-NINE

E mily...
     The minute he used the phrase I'd only read in books was the moment I knew I was his, body and soul. Something about those two little words flipped something inside me, and I gave him everything I had. He worked me up, winding me tighter and tighter, only to back off and let the pressure fade before starting all over again.

After entirely too long, and what was likely far less time than it felt like, he let me fall, carefree, into absolute bliss. Wave after wave crashed over me, and I was drowning in the ecstasy he'd created, a place I didn't ever want to leave. When I found my way back to shore, he was there, holding me tight, keeping me safe in the beautiful storm he'd thrown me into.

"Hmm," I hummed, unable to form words.

"Ready for a bath?" he asked.

I shook my head, so he smoothed his hands up my side, his lips pressed against my temple. It didn't take long for me to get chilled, and when I shivered, he scooped me up and walked to the bathroom, setting me on the toilet that had its own little room within, closing the door behind him to let me have my privacy.

The water turned on, so I knew he was drawing a bath, and I smiled. I couldn't remember anyone but my mom ever doing this kind of thing for me. Not the sex, cause that would be disgusting, but taking care of me, seeing my needs before I voiced them, and taking charge to make it happen. It was all so much I could barely hold it in.

Instead of fighting it, though, I let myself feel. Feel how my life was falling apart, how my career had imploded in an instant, and how this man, who I saw as the chance to get ahead if I used him right, gave me more than I ever could have hoped for. If anyone would've asked me where I saw myself on this day a couple months ago, I'd never in my wildest dreams thought this would be it.

"Hey," he said with a soft knock on the door. "You okay?"

"Yeah," I said, letting myself pee before wiping and flushing.

I opened the door, and his blue eyes held something in them I couldn't quite read. It could be concern, fear, or something I didn't have a name for. Before I had time to even try to analyze it, it was gone. His hand slid along my chin, hooking the back of my neck and pulling me toward him. Wrapped in his arms was a place I was growing to love, and that terrified me. I wasn't in a position to be in a relationship, no matter how simple this one seemed.

"Come on," he said, steering me toward the tub.

The lights in the room were low, and I wondered how he'd managed that, but I didn't want to think too hard on it, as it really wasn't that important in the grand scheme of things. He held my hand as I lifted first one, then the other leg over the tub's edge, settling myself in among the bubbles covering the surface. The lavender scent surrounded me, and it was such a relaxing feeling.

"Too hot?" he asked. "Too much?"

"Not at all," I said, reaching a hand up to help him in.

"Hang on," he said, stepping out of the bathroom.

When he came back in, he was holding one of the cups they had on the counter in the room, and it was filled with those Dove chocolates. The little blue wrappers were unmistakable, and I wondered how and when he'd gotten them.

"I hope this is all right," he said, setting the cup on the edge of the tub. "I had someone help me out. With the bath things and the chocolate."

There was a wistfulness in the way he said it, and I wasn't quite sure what to make of it, so I didn't bother to try and dissect it.

"It's perfect," I said.

His smile lit his face, showing a dimple I'd not seen before. He climbed into the tub, then settled in behind me, his legs around mine, pulling me back against his front with his arms around my waist. It was intimate but not at all sexual. Well, not overtly so, anyway. Grabbing the cup from the edge of the tub, he held it in front of me, and I looked around, not wanting to get the suds on the chocolate.

"Here," he said, setting the cup down and reaching behind him.

I wiped my hands on the hand towel he'd held for me, and then he set it on the edge, carefully keeping the edges out of the water. Again, he brought the cup to me, and I pulled out a piece of chocolate, being careful when I opened it that I didn't drop it into the tub. As I put it in my mouth, I relished in the sweetness, letting it dissolve on my tongue, enjoying its simplicity of it.

"Good?" he asked, his voice hushed in the soft atmosphere we'd found ourselves in.

"So good," I said, reaching over to take another piece.

I opened it up, then shifted, holding it out for him to take in his mouth. He did, his lips wrapped around my fingers as I let it go on his tongue.

"Chocolate," he said around the piece. "With just a hint of Emily. My favorite."

"Goofball," I said, settling back against his chest.

With his arms around my middle, my head resting on his shoulder, and the quietness of the space, I felt more at peace than I had in entirely too long. I wondered if I'd tried to do too much, push too hard, and expect everything I wanted quickly. If so, what would slowing down look like? Would it mean giving up everything or choosing what I wanted to do?

There were so many possibilities for me, and yet, nothing seemed like it was something that was worth fighting for. Hell, even the job with the station had a sour taste to it, especially since we realized that the owner had some sort of vendetta against me. It wasn't certain, but it seemed pretty obvious. The thing I didn't understand was why? What had I done to get on his bad side? Was it simply because I was a woman? Or was there something more that I wasn't aware of?

"Stop thinking," Silas said. "Your brain is too loud. It's not letting you relax."

I took a deep breath, held it, and then let it out, the flow of air moving the bubbles on the surface of the water.

"Good girl," he said.

I settled back against him further, letting go of the what-ifs that had been racing through my brain. Tomorrow would be soon enough to look closer at them. Right now, I had a strong set of arms wrapped around me, and the world could wait.

CHAPTER FIFTY

S ilas...
When she finally let go of whatever was running through her brain and relaxed, so did I. There was so much we needed to deal with, but for this one night, I wanted it to be left at the door. When we walked out in the morning, it would still be there. The warm water, the scent of flowers, and the taste of chocolate had me in a happy place, and I didn't want to disturb it.

As the water cooled, I shifted her, rubbing the suds and water all over her skin, making sure to take advantage of whatever it was that was in that bath thing Sue helped me pick out. She'd been the perfect person to meet in the middle of a grocery store aisle, and I hoped she took advantage of the card I gave her. But she wasn't the woman I should have on my mind, so I let the thought go and continued to rub the one in the tub with me.

"Come on," she said, shifting away from me. "Let's make use of that bed again."

"Your wish is my command," I said, standing up and grabbing towels from the rack on the wall.

She stepped out of the tub, took the towel, and wrapped it

around her, picking up the cup of chocolate as she stepped back to give me room. The cup went on the counter, and she rubbed her body with the towel, drying herself off. I wondered how that simple act could be such a fucking turn-on, because it was just so normal. I dried quickly, not really caring if I left the sheets wet, then took the towel from her and finished the job, making sure I caressed every part of her.

"You're handy to have around," she said.

"Glad you think so," I replied.

Scooping her up, she giggled but reached around to grab the cup with the chocolate. As I walked to the bed, she opened another piece, pressing it between my lips as I took it in. When I stood her up, she pulled me down and kissed me hard. I opened my mouth to share the piece with her. Never in my wildest dreams would I think to share food in that way, but it was so fucking erotic that I didn't want to stop.

"You taste good covered in chocolate," she said, stepping back just a bit.

"You taste good no matter what," I replied, licking my lips. "I want to taste every inch of you over and over again. And I'm gonna start with that hot, wet pussy."

Shoving her over onto the bed, she gasped, then moaned as I followed her, my mouth on her pussy, just as I'd promised. I licked and nipped at her, pressing her legs apart so I could get as much of her exposed as possible. When I slid a finger inside her, she clenched around it, her body shivering. I added another finger, sliding them in and out while pressing on her clit with my thumb. With her legs up and over my shoulders, I could easily get to her ass as well, and I let my tongue do the exploring, the opening puckering and clenching right along with her cunt.

Her breathing became more erratic, and her fists clenched in the blankets, so I increased the tempo, shifting to a more come-hither motion with my fingers, scratching that patch just inside her. I moved my tongue to work on her clit, and slipped a finger from my other hand inside her pussy, gathering up her essence before sliding it down to her ass and pressing on the opening. She clenched but then relaxed, taking a deep breath before letting it out, bearing down to allow my finger to slide in.

I worked her slowly, more focused on her clit and pussy, just using pressure in her ass, and her body reacted beautifully. I could see her nipples pebble, becoming tight nubs at the tip of her breasts, and when she moved her hands up to massage them, then pull on the tips, I moved my finger in her ass more, sliding it in and out in time with the strokes I was using on her pussy. Her stomach sucked in, spasming, and I could feel her tightening around my fingers, so I knew she was close. Sucking her clit into my mouth, I set my teeth into it just enough to give more than just pressure, and she exploded.

Her whole body tensed, her back arched, and her fingers pulled her tits so tight it looked painful. The entire time, her thighs were slammed against my head, her pussy sucking my fingers in, and her ass tight around my other one. She stopped breathing, her whole body one big, tight spring until she spasmed again, letting out a long, low groan as she came down from wherever it was she'd flown off to.

The sight was exquisite, and I never wanted it to end. If I could, I'd give her orgasms like that all day, every day. But the world outside these walls would come crashing through at some point, so my task for tonight was to make her forget everything else. So far, it seemed to be working.

"Holy," she whispered, the air rushing out of her. "Fuck."

She'd relaxed enough that I could pull myself free of her, and I stood up, looking at the absolutely perfect mess she'd become. Her hair was tangled but seemed to float around her head. Her eyes were glassy as if they were looking through some starlight filter. Her cheeks were pink, her lips were swollen, and her breasts were red from her attention to the nipples. She was the picture of perfection, and I felt a bit proud that I'd given her that look.

"Gonna go wash up," I said.

"Be quick," she replied.

I went to the sink and washed my hands, making sure they were completely clean. When I was sure, I turned the water off and then headed back to the bed. She'd shifted herself up to the pillows and shoved the blankets and sheets down, lying there waiting.

"Come here," she said, reaching a hand out.

I did as she said, walking to the bed and climbing in next to her. Her hand found my cock, stroking it from base to tip, giving a twist at the top before sliding back down. The bit of precum that had leaked out helped her slide easily, and she stroked me while she stared right into my eyes. As I got harder, she went faster, but I wasn't gonna go with just her hand. It wasn't anything to do with her. I just knew I wouldn't get there.

"Fuck me," she said, shifting so she was on her back, urging me to get on top of her.

My cock seemed to have a homing device in it because it found her warm wet center easily, sliding in without any assistance. Even though she'd come so violently a few minutes ago, she was still tight around me. I began to move, slow and deep, pulling almost all the way out before sliding back in. Her hips rose to meet me with each stroke, not trying to rush me in any way.

After a bit, I started to move faster, and she shifted her hips, raising her leg up a bit. My arm went behind it, pushing it toward her chest, giving me a deeper thrust into her. Her eyes widened, her mouth forming a perfect "O" as I hit that spot inside. Picking up the pace even further, I pulled back farther, slamming against her harder and harder, her breath kicking up a notch every few strokes.

"Oh, yes," she said as she pulled her leg farther up. "Harder. Faster. Fuck me."

Not one to hold back and always up for a challenge, I did just what she said, fucking her harder and faster, and with the angle of her body, deeper with each stroke. Her pussy clenched around me, and that tingling hit my spine. When she screamed out my name, I lost my control, letting everything I had loose inside her, stroke after stroke, pumping my cum inside her body.

I collapsed down on top of her, shifting to the side to not put my full weight on her body as I tried to figure out how to breathe again. Her arms wrapped around me, pulling me back on top of her, and I went without a fight. The feel of her warm, sweat-slicked body under me was the only place I wanted to be. I could die happy in that moment because I felt like I'd connected with her on more than just a physical level. There was intimacy, and then there was whatever had happened between us in that moment.

"MORNING," she said, and her warm, pliant body next to me had me needing her.

"Morning," I replied, my voice scratchy with sleep.

"We need to talk," she said, and that woke me right the fuck up.

"Okay," I said, opening my eyes and looking at her. I couldn't read her expression, so I had no idea what she was gonna say, or where this was gonna go.

"We made a mistake," she said, her eyes not meeting mine.

"How so?" I asked.

"You didn't wear a condom," she said, and the realization hit me right in the fucking face.

"Shit," I said. "God damn. Fuck."

"Hey," she said, her hand on my cheek. "I'm clean."

"I am, too," I said. "But I can get you the morning-after pill or whatever you need if you want. I didn't mean to. I would never do that on purpose."

"It's fine," she said. "I'm on the pill. I just wanted you to know, you know?"

"Okay," I said. "You sure you're okay? 'Cause it's okay if you're not."

"No," she said. "I'm fine. It'll be fine. I'm sure it's fine."

"Now you're worried," I said.

"I'm not," she said.

"What do we do if…"

Fuck, I didn't even want to think the thought, let alone voice it. Afraid if I said it out loud, it would make it true.

"We figure it out," she said.

"You sure?"

"Would you stop asking me that?" she said.

"I fucked it up," I said. "I'm the one who's at fault. If you want me to leave, I will. Fuck, I'll never talk to you again if that's what you want."

"Would you shut up?" she said, pressing her lips to mine.

Her body wrapped around me, and she climbed on top of me, straddling me and letting her warm, wet pussy slide up and down my cock. Fuck, she was hot in every way I needed, and I had gone and fucked everything up by not wrapping my shit up. Except, she seemed to not give two shits about it, and from the way she was moving, it seemed like she was more than willing to deal with the risks a second time. I grabbed her hips, stilling her movement, and she pulled her mouth from mine, looking down into my eyes with a mix of confusion and fear.

"I'm not gonna push you," I said. "But I want you to be

sure this is what you want. Don't do it because it's already been done."

"I want this," she said. "I want us. I know it's too soon, and I fucking know it's stupid, but I don't fucking care right now. I want you more than I've wanted anything in my life. Fuck, even more than my desire to be in front of the camera. There isn't anything I covet right now that compares to how much I want this."

It was a lot, but I'd been thinking it while we were in the tub, so I guess we were both on the same page. She was beautiful, strong, smart, and more than I thought I'd ever deserve in this life. And she was willingly handing it all to me. All I had to do was take the gift.

"Yeah?" I said softly.

"Yeah?" she asked.

I paused, thought about it again, and nodded.

"Yeah," I said, with more force this time. "Fuck, yeah. I want this, you, everything. I want to take care of you, protect you, and give you everything I have. Let's do this."

Her mouth crashed into mine so hard it jarred me. I grabbed the back of her neck and held her there, then slid a hand around to her ass and flipped us over, taking the driver's seat, plunging my tongue into her mouth as I shifted to plunge my cock into her pussy. Her legs wrapped around my waist, holding me to her as I pumped in and out of her faster than I had before, feeling the build-up in her as it did in me until we both exploded, her going first and me right after, chasing her across the universe.

EPILOGUE

APRIL...

Emily...

It was the first game of the first round of the Stanley Cup Playoffs, and we were at home. Sitting against the glass, right by the penalty box, I tightly wrapped my jacket around me. My entire life had changed in just six short months, and there was no way I could have predicted this outcome. Still, I wouldn't have wanted to change much of it. At least not the parts that I shared with Silas.

"Austin, number thirteen, has a two-minute penalty for high sticking," the ref said, and I shook my head.

"Hey, baby," Silas said as he climbed into the box.

"Did you get a penalty just to come see me?" I asked.

"Maybe," he said, his smile wide.

"Don't do it again," I shouted as the crowd got loud around me.

Turning to look at the ice, I watched Fahn slap the puck into the net, the light going off with the goal.

"I'm gonna miss you," Silas said as he headed out of the box.

"Don't come back," I shouted, but I couldn't help but smile.

Watching him glide on the ice was mesmerizing, and I didn't think I'd ever tire of it. The power he used to move lightning fast was something I could never aspire to, and the way he had no fear when chasing down the puck or a player who'd hit one of his guys made the butterflies in my stomach go crazy.

The team had purchased the cable station, and Joe Davidson was brought up on some serious charges, including stalking not just me but several women who worked for the station. He'd kept most of us on the hook, promising a bigger presence on the station, so long as we jumped through the ever-changing hoops he placed in front of us.

What pissed me off the most, though, was the fact that he'd orchestrated Gregory coming back into my life. It was never really clear how he did it, but somehow, he'd gotten in contact with him, convinced him that I wanted him back and that he had to use a firm hand with me because that's what I was into. It's just too bad he couldn't be charged with the guy's death. I had to go through a shit ton of therapy to help me realize that it wasn't my fault and that the part I played in his death wasn't really on my head at all. It was just a freak accident. There were still days it haunted me, but each session with my therapist moved me toward a better place mentally.

Watching the men on the ice skate around, shove each other into the walls, and slap the puck back and forth with such precision, all while gliding on a razor's edge under their feet, was inspiring. Maybe those genes would be passed along to the little one I had growing inside me. I hadn't told Silas yet because I didn't want to distract him. Besides, he'd be even more protective of me than he already was.

"He's so fast," Sue said.

She'd become a part of our lives rather quickly. My heart

melted when Silas told me about her helping him in the store. The way he talked about her, how she reminded him of his mom, and that she'd been the one to help him put together the little package he'd gotten for me, was just perfect.

We got married on Christmas Day, and it was the best gift I'd ever received. It was super fast in the relationship, but it felt right, too. My brothers all hassled me about marrying a hockey player, but they seemed to get along well with Silas. They appreciated the way he'd protected me and taken care of me. They just didn't like that he played a terrible sport. When he'd challenged them to a skate-off, they all backed off pretty quickly, which made me laugh.

"It's amazing how they all stay upright on those things," I said. "Silas tried to get me to skate once, but he spent more time on his ass with me on top of him than he liked. He deemed me unsafe to skate with, which was fine with me."

"He's so good with you," she said. "I can't wait to see how he reacts to your news."

I hadn't told her I was pregnant. She'd sussed it out pretty quickly on her own. I'd sworn her to secrecy, and she said she would never ruin that surprise. She was the only person besides the doctor and me to know, and since it had only been a couple weeks, it was our little secret. She'd even started a cute little blanket with the blue and gold colors of the team bordering it and a hockey stick and puck in the middle. She planned to save it in a closet where her husband never looked.

He'd come to a few of the games but said the cold of the stadium hurt his knees. I went to their place sometimes to watch the away games, though, and he was an enthusiastic fan, so I didn't begrudge him for staying away from the arena.

We had made a plan that when the team lost the last game of the season or won the whole thing, I would insist on Silas going with me to their house so they could give him a gift as either a congratulation or commiseration. He didn't know the plan, and Sue's husband only knew there was one. I almost wanted them to lose quickly so I could tell him, but I knew that would break his heart. My only concern was whether I could hold out long enough and keep the secret to the very end.

The crash against the glass brought me back to the present, and Silas had one of the other team's players pinned to the wall, his stick sliding around them, trying to get the puck out. When it went, he turned and winked at me before flying across the ice to help one of his teammates find the goal.

Back and forth the puck went, the men flying up and down the ice as they fought for dominance and the win. When the final buzzer sounded, we had won, and I was thrilled, cheering along with the rest of the crowd.

As much as I fought to get in front of the camera, I found that the piece I'd put together on Silas, the tour of his house, and the interview we finally sat down and finished was where my true heart sat. I wanted to get to know the people I talked with, to find out what made them tick and what drove them to be the best they were at their chosen sport. Having talked with Lily, the woman who was doing the documentary, I realized that I didn't need to be tied to one station, one team, or even one sport.

When I finally uploaded my piece, it hit everywhere. It was picked up by the local stations, the cable network ran it, and someone from ESPN even asked to show it on their network as part of some series they wanted to do. The revenue from just that one piece gave me enough money to not have to worry about every penny I spent. Silas promised to take care of me, but I wanted to be an equal partner in our relationship. Wanted to contribute just as much as he did.

"I fucking love you," he shouted from the ice when he'd finished with the game-ending formalities.

"Language," Sue said, her motherly instincts showing. "There are children around."

"Sorry," he said, looking like he meant it. "Be done in a minute," he added, looking at me like he wanted to devour me.

After he skated off, Sue rubbed my shoulder, a smile on her face.

"I know that look," she said. "If you weren't already, you know," she said, her eyes looking down at my belly. "Well, then, I wouldn't be surprised if you were after tonight."

"You're terrible," I said, but I couldn't help but smile.

When Silas came out of the dressing room, he scooped me up, arms around my back, and held me tight as he kissed me. Then he put me down, kissed my forehead, and held me against his chest. The ride home was quick, and when we walked in the door, he spun me around, pressing my back against the closed door.

"You've been keeping secrets," he said. "I'm not mad, though. I can't wait to meet her."

"What are you talking about?" I asked, wondering how he found out.

"That baby that's growing in your belly," he said. "She's gonna be beautiful, just like her mama. And she isn't gonna date until she's at least thirty. No, forty. Maybe fifty."

"What if it's a boy?" I asked, giving him the answer to the unasked question.

"Then he better be born with a pair of skates on," he said. "'Cause he's gonna learn fast how to be a brawler."

"Will you let your daughter be a brawler?" I asked because I wouldn't let him exclude a daughter if she wanted to play hockey.

"Oh," he said like that thought hadn't occurred to him.

"Yeah. It'll be sure to keep the guys away from her. They'll be terrified."

"Especially if she's like her daddy," I said.

"Her daddy," he mimicked, trying the title on. "I can't wait."

NOTE FROM AUTHOR

Images and Blurbs available upon request.
I would ask that you obtain high quality headshots and cover art images directly through me, rather than taking them from either my website or Amazon, however, blurbs are readily available through both places.

ABOUT THE AUTHOR

Born and raised in the Pacific Northwest, CM Kane was fed a steady diet of sports, particularly baseball. Having this love of the game instilled in her at an early age, she found that nothing was better than getting lost in the game. Storytelling was another gift that was encouraged in her youth, and she's taking to the written word to explore a new aspect to the game she loves.

Social Media and Website Links:

Website:
https://www.authorcmkane.com

Facebook:
https://www.facebook.com/AuthorCMKane

Instagram:
https://www.instagram.com/authorcmkane/

Amazon:
https://www.amazon.com/author/cmkane

BlueSky:
https://bsky.app/profile/authorcmkane.bsky.social

ALSO BY C.M. KANE

Seattle Cascades

1. Extra Innings

2. Caught Stealing

3. Backstop

4. Power Hitter

5. Double Play

5.5. Find a Gap

6. Sweet Spot (Coming Soon)

7. 7th Inning Stretch (Coming Soon)

New Orleans Magicians

1. Choke Up

2. Caught in a Pickle

3. Brand New Ballgame (Coming Soon)

4. Fan Interference (Coming Soon)

5. Flashing the Leather (Coming Soon)

Austin Aces Hockey Club (Shared World)

Power Play

Anthologies

Unnerving: Eclipse

Street Justice (Limited Time)

Fooling Around (Coming April 1, 2025)

Neon Lights & Country Nights (Coming June 1, 2025)

Stand Alone Titles

A Switch in Time